THE DAY SHE DIED
by Helen Reilly

Inspector McKee of Manhattan Homicide, on a holiday, is driving from Denver to Albuquerque when overtaken by a violent spring storm. His car disabled, he makes for refuge in an isolated old hacienda. In the courtyard he finds a Mexican lying with his head bashed in. Without so much as a by-your-leave, he drags the dying man in and gets him to bed, commandeering the help of such people as he finds. In the ranch-house appear, one by one, a strangely assorted group: its brassy lady tenant; a mousey little woman who pretends to be a stranger here; a New York broker with his fiancée and her sister; and a corset salesman from Chicago. All seemingly have something to hide; the Inspector vainly tries to figure out what.

As the storm becomes a flood, the atmosphere grows creepier; strangers in a ghostly house, suspicious of each other; evidence of prowlers and secret searches. Soon McKee discovers the corpse of a young woman in one of the outbuildings; a shocking murder has been committed—two if the Mexican dies. But many clues only mock him, because they fail to connect the two deeds of violence.

He does ascertain that the ranch had been owned by the Dane sisters; that the older, Veronica, was now dead; and that the younger, Mary, had just recently rented the place to a Mrs. Fergusson. When the storm abates and the authorities arrive, McKee, far out of his jurisdiction, agrees to help them. They unveil an old love affair, the failure of a woman in her attempt to play God, and the surprising face of guilt.

Mrs. Reilly's final mystery, set against a romantic Southwestern background, is one of the most devious in structure, and satisfying in solution, she ever wrote.

THE DAY SHE DIED

Recent Books by Helen Reilly

THE
DAY
SHE DIED

by Helen Reilly

RANDOM HOUSE

New York

THE DAY SHE DIED

I

It was at Headquarters, in Commissioner Carey's office on the second floor of the great gray building on Centre Street that Christopher McKee, head of Homicide East, first heard Veronica Dane's name. He heard it from his friend, Fernandez, New York's Chief Medical Examiner. The two men were waiting for the Commissioner, and Fernandez who had been born and brought up in the Southwest had picked up an Albuquerque newspaper and was glancing through it, lounging in a chair, a leg thrown over the arm.

The story was on the second page as well as in the obits. The family was widely known and highly respected in that part of the country; it had numbered statesmen, a governor, an ambassador and several senators among its members. Fernandez dropped the paper. "By George," he exclaimed, "Veronica Dane dead, of natural causes—I always thought someone would kill her."

He gave his head a half-amused, half-rueful shake. "What a woman, McKee, big, strapping, handsome, and as strong as an ox. She could drive a plow or a four-in-hand with equal ease—and dash. The last time I was out there two years ago she was thinking of buying a plane if she could get hold of the money . . . 'Of natural causes' . . . Well, I'd have given her another twenty years myself."

McKee blew smoke lazily and watched it rise in the dusk of the big room. "Doesn't sound like a prospective victim to me. Why did you think someone would kill the lady?"

Fernandez shrugged. "Human flesh and blood can stand just so much . . . Veronica was a matriarch to end all matriarchs—the boss. Over the years she ground everyone around her to powder: her father, although the old man would never admit it, she was his pride and joy; her mother, a brother and a younger sister, Mary . . . Oh well, she's gone. Not exactly what you'd call a lovable character but an impressive one. I suppose I'll have to send a wreath . . ."

The Commissioner came in then and the subject was dropped.

Fernandez's wreath duly arrived at the Dane ranch, El Toro, in northern New Mexico among other tributes from far away sent by people who had once been friends of the Danes, and Veronica was duly buried in the family graveyard on the estate with full benefit of clergy and a scant handful of local people in attendance. The Dane fortunes were on the wane and they had kept themselves to themselves for the last few years. They were proud people—or at least Veronica Dane had been.

Her sudden passing had given rise to neither questions nor surprise. She was a woman in her late sixties, her blood pressure was high, and she had absolutely refused to obey her doctor's orders. Consequently she had died as a result of a stroke. There was no one with her. She was alone in the immense old house at the time. The only servants, the yardman and the cook, were at a fiesta in Las Cruces—

Veronica had graciously given them the day off—and Mary Dane was shopping in Albuquerque. It was Mary who had found her older sister, slumped down in her chair at the stately dining-room table, an untasted cup of tea on a lace doily in front of her. Her hands were at her throat, the fingers caught under the black velvet ribbon she wore round her neck. She had evidently been trying to loosen it when death struck.

Arriving in response to Mary's frantic call, the doctor assured the younger woman that even if she had been at home it wouldn't have made any difference, there was nothing she could have done. He had more or less expected it to happen and he signed the death certificate and went his way without further ado.

Then the countryside did get a surprise. Denuded as El Toro was of its former splendor, its pomp and circumstance and many of its acres, Veronica Dane had loved the ranch passionately. Five days after the funeral it was put up for sale, lock, stock and barrel.

Mary, grief-stricken and confused as she was and her own mistress for the first time in her life, was positive of just one thing. She wasn't going to stay on at El Toro a day more than she could help. Her vehemence startled Tony Santander, the family lawyer, when she came to his office in Albuquerque three days after the funeral. Santander had admired and feared Veronica, he was fond of Mary. She was not a woman anyone would be afraid of. In her late fifties she was round and plump and pleasing, with soft blue eyes, a quiet voice and a gentle manner.

"I can't stand it, Tony," she said with unusual force. "It's so *lonely* without Vero, you have no idea . . . And I'm scared at night. Yes, I know it sounds queer but I am. I keep thinking I hear things, the next thing will be that I'll be seeing them . . . Everything is completely different, everything. Vero's pet dog Spot's gone—he simply disappeared, and Carlo, the horse she liked so much, the one she raised from a colt, won't let me get anywhere near him."

"But you have your cook, Della, and the yardman, Mary," Santander said.

"Emilio sleeps in the stable when he's there at all nights—he goes to his sister a lot—and Della's in her room off the kitchen, miles away. I could be killed or die of fright and they wouldn't know about it until morning." She pressed her hands together nervously in her lap. "I want to get rid of the place as soon as possible even if it's at a sacrifice. I don't care."

If she wanted to she could. On their mother's death the ranch had been left jointly to Veronica and Mary and was to go to the survivor. It was Mary's outright now and she could do what she pleased. But El Toro hadn't been a working ranch in a good many years and it was rapidly reverting to its original wild state. The fences were in bad repair, the cleared fields choking up with piñons and sage. As for the stock, once extensive, it consisted now of some chickens—Veronica had liked a fresh egg with her tea— a couple of horses, a cow and a calf and various dogs and cats. The house itself, one of the most ancient haciendas in the state, had been well built and was still in fair shape, although too antiquated for modern tastes and with an old-fashioned kitchen—that bête noire of the present-day housewife.

Santander warned Mary Dane not to get her hopes up, that the chances of a quick sale were dim. But she was very much in earnest and he put an ad in the local Albuquerque papers and in the Denver *Post* without, however, much optimism. Then, unexpectedly, at the end of the week a buyer turned up.

An Easterner, a Mrs. Fergusson from Chicago, offered for El Toro, but with a proviso attached. The proviso was that she rent El Toro for six months with an option to buy if she found the place suited. Her husband was in the East settling up his affairs, and the final decision would have to wait on him.

Mrs. Fergusson was a woman somewhere in her forties with an excellent well-girdled figure, a hard eye, a lot of make-up and plenty of assurance. Her clothes were good, and the rings and long dangling earrings she wore were valuable. She was definitely a city dweller. She explained that she was thinking of writing a book and needed quiet, and that her husband had it in mind to settle down, they had traveled a lot, and that he'd like to do a bit of farming. Not much, just enough to amuse himself and keep him busy. She gave as references two banks, one in Phoenix and the other in Chicago, with both of which Santander checked. For some reason or other, although the woman was pleasant enough, and seemed to know her own mind, Santander didn't like her. But the money was O.K. and he forwarded the offer, which was a fair one, to Mary Dane.

Mary promptly accepted it, proviso and all. She didn't care who she sold the ranch to, all she wanted was to get rid of it and get away. Mrs. Fergusson paid over the six months' rent in advance, and a thousand dollars down for the option, the papers were signed and the deal closed, and on the second of March Mary moved out of El Toro and Mrs. Fergusson moved in.

Mary herself was going to stay with some rancher friends four miles to the east for a month or so, until she found out what she wanted to do. She was grieved that Mrs. Fergusson didn't intend to keep on either Della or Emilio, the latter of whom had been with the family for a long while. She said her husband would be bringing on their own maid from Chicago in a few days, meanwhile she wouldn't need anyone. "You won't be afraid?" Mary hazarded. Mrs. Fergusson was amused. "My dear Miss Dane, why should I be?"

The house was fully furnished and well stocked with necessities. There was a deep-freeze in the stable and a

cold room in an outbuilding close by. Home-cured hams
and flitches of bacon hung from the rafters, together with
venison, half a yearling, and a couple of sides of beef.

Most of the really valuable things in the hacienda had
long ago been sold. Mary took only her own personal belongings with her. The few relics that remained were
locked in a cupboard in the dining room for collection
later when she decided where she was going to settle down
permanently. "I'll run over then myself and pick them up,
or have someone else collect them."

Mrs. Fergusson wasn't unpleasant about the locked
dining-room cupboard, there was plenty of storage space
in the house, in fact she smiled sweetly. But she was crisp
and incisive.

"When you do want to come and get your things
you'll be sure and let me know well in advance, won't you,
Miss Dane? I haven't been well, I had an operation two
months ago and I need rest and quiet—and besides I might
be out if I wasn't warned beforehand." Mary said of
course. She surrendered a complete set of door keys with
the exception of the one for the locked closet, said good-bye
and closed the front door behind her for the last time.

Bill Speaker, the owner of the ranch where she was
going to stay, with him and his wife, was waiting in the
corral under the Chinese elms around at the side with the
pick-up truck, her bags already stowed in the back. Bill
was watching the horses in the corral curiously, or rather
Veronica's stallion, Carlo. "He's as nervous as a witch," he
said. "Wonder what's wrong, what's got under his skin?
Look at him run, just look at him—and his ears are back."

"I know." Mary settled herself beside him. "I think
he misses Vero. He's been like that ever since Vero died.
And then there's Spot, too."

"The Dalmatian?"

"Yes. Vero raised him from a pup. He was one of
Juno's litter. He's never appeared, you know, since that

day. He wasn't around when I came home and found her . . ." She sighed. "Emilio'll be over later to take the two horses and Betsey and her calf, and those three strays and the cats. Mrs. Fergusson doesn't want them—she doesn't seem to like animals."

"Tough-looking babe if you ask me," Bill Speaker said with a grin. "Got her nerve with her. Doesn't look as though she's ever been in the country before in her life. She'll learn—she'll probably be overrun with rats in no time flat. Oh, well, not your funeral, Mary. Yes, the lady'll learn." He started the engine, backed around, and they drove off under the elms and cottonwoods through the milky sunlight and crisp air. There was no sign of bad weather then, except for a slight haze and a few drifting clouds over the tops of the Sandias ringing the valley on all sides. It was a little after one o'clock that they went through the El Toro gates and swung east.

A short time later in Denver, three hundred miles to the north, an assemblage of officials from twenty-four states was winding up the order of business, which was a discussion of ways and means of crime prevention. Christopher McKee of the New York Homicide Bureau was among those present, representing his city. The Commissioner was to have come but something had turned up at the last moment and he had drafted McKee instead. The Scotsman was to have flown back that night but the weather was worsening rapidly over the Rockies, and all night flights east had been canceled.

"You could," someone suggested, "get down to Phoenix and probably get a jet out of there."

But McKee had made other plans. He was in no particular hurry, they had wound up the session early and a day or so either way wasn't important. At the moment there was nothing at the office in New York that required his personal attention and as soon as his flight was wiped out

he had called Colonel James Ringrose. The Colonel was
an old army friend of his who had settled down on a ranch
near Santa Teresa in western New Mexico. Ringrose had
pressed McKee to come and pay himself and his wife a
visit countless times. "Come out and take a sniff of our
mile-high air and see how a free man lives," he had urged
again and again both by letter and on an occasional trip
east. "I'll give you the best venison steak you could sink a
tooth in—and as for fish . . ."

It hadn't been possible before, the distance was too
long. But the Scotsman was fond of old James and now that
he was out here anyhow, this was his opportunity. He ar-
ranged for a drive-yourself car at the desk and early the
next morning he started south.

Even with the worsening weather, if he had stuck to
the main road he wouldn't have got into any serious trouble.
But over the phone the night before, Ringrose had given
him detailed instructions for a shorter route that would save
a lot of mileage and give them a longer time together.
Taking this route was where McKee made his mistake. It
was sleeting when he left Denver, snowing in the mountain
passes. After the snow the mist came, and following the
mist, the wind and the rain.

McKee was used to wind in New York and rain also,
but not such rain and wind as he ran into making his way
southwest. After he put Santa Fe behind him, turning off at
a tangent, it got steadily worse. Half a dozen times he was
all but blown off the road into a yawning valley hundreds
of feet below. The rain was no longer ordinary rain, it had
become a howling Niagara of solid water. All the land-
marks Ringrose had described were wiped out and by
four o'clock he was hopelessly lost. The road he was following was narrow, winding and precipitous. Up and down;
it cut through gorges, climbed into the invisible sky and
plunged as abruptly into unseen depths.

To stop would be fatal. He had no idea of where he was. Even his sense of direction, ordinarily excellent, had deserted him. It got dark early and after dark he met no other cars. There were no towns or settlements, or at least none that he could see. And there wasn't even the glimmer of a light in a distant house, nothing but here and there a swift glimpse of a huddle of sheep or cattle in a hollow. The only thing to do was to keep on fighting south and west as nearly as he could figure in the hope either of running out of the storm or eventually reaching civilization of some sort.

He knew he was in the Sandias, from their height and their position on the map, and that was all he did know. As he got farther into them, tree branches began to litter the slimy surface of the roadbed, washboarded and pitted with holes you could throw a Saint Bernard in, and rounding a hairpin turn he came on a telegraph pole hanging crookedly in a tangle of torn wires. It was pitch-black by half-past four. The rain was freezing in spots as it fell, the windshield wipers were useless, and after a while McKee was forced to drive with his head out the window, eyes half closed against the stinging slash of the near sleet.

Instead of getting better the going got gradually worse. And there was another alarming development. In the low spots, stony bottoms and gorges between the mountains and mesas, the road was under water pouring down from arroyos recently dry and now great rushing torrents. He made one rickety wooden bridge with inches to spare before it slewed drunkenly and was swept from its moorings practically under his hind wheels.

McKee would have stopped then and sweated it out for the night except that he knew from Fernandez that in the early spring these storms sometimes went on for days on end. So he kept going, lurching over unseen obstacles and skidding from side to side and in and out of

ruts in mud that was becoming dangerously deep and that
was as slippery as hell—it was like driving through a bottomless pond of glue.

The end of his progress came suddenly. A faint cry
above the roar of the wind and the rain, a dim figure directly in his path; it was a man. The Scotsman gave the
wheel a sharp twist and stood on the brake. The car
promptly slammed sideways across the road into a wall of
rock. A jolt, the shrieking of metal and the crash of glass.
The headlamps were gone. There was a flashlight in the
glove compartment. McKee felt for it, switched it on and
leaped out.

There was no prostrate body lying ominously on the
ground. The man he had almost run down had managed
to jump out of the way. He was stumbling to his feet,
plastered liberally with mud. He swayed drunkenly, wiped
his face with a gloved hand and stared at McKee in the
sudden flood of light. He looked exhausted. He was an
Easterner from his clothes, what you could see of them;
in his early forties, with an ugly clever-looking face and
bare head. He had apparently lost his hat. His hair was
plastered to his skull with rain.

They had to shout at each other to make themselves
heard above the din. The man's name was Steele, and
they were both in the same case, both lost and both with
their cars done for. Temporarily at least. McKee's car
was out of commission and Steele's was upside down in a
ditch a hundred feet farther along. "Where are we?"
Steele shouted, and McKee shrugged and shouted back,
"Search me," and sent his flash swinging.

They were on fairly level ground in some sort of
valley. Low serrated red cliffs down which water was
pouring hemmed the road in on one side. On the other,
beyond bushes beaten almost flat, a cow gazed at them from
behind a barbed-wire fence with a stupid bemused face.
It lowed at them mournfully. Barbed wire meant a farm

or ranch . . . The two men followed the wire south, slipping and sliding in the thick mud, rain beating down on them in sheets, for almost half a mile. The wire fence ended at stone gateposts and the mouth of a driveway. There was an iron arch over the stone pillars, linking them together. There was a name in faded gilt letters on the arching bow of iron. McKee recognized it. Fernandez and the Commissioner's office . . . The name of the ranch was El Toro, only the O was gone. The name Dane was also on a mailbox on a post close to the road.

The two men turned in through the gates and advanced up the driveway, mud sucking at their feet so thick it all but pulled their shoes off. It was laborious going. The flashlight picked out trees, elms and cottonwoods, and glimpses of cleared fields on either hand, but no house. There was nothing but the roar of the wind and the flailing rain. Then there was another sound. It was the muffled clop of hoofs.

The Scotsman sent light forward. A man was galloping down the driveway toward them on a big black horse. He was riding bareback. He pulled up as he neared them, imprisoned in the circle of light.

The rider was tall and lean and young, scarcely out of his teens, if that. He wore a khaki windbreaker, dungarees and boots. He looked frightened. His eyes glittered in a wet white face. It was a good face, open, attractive. He was the first to speak.

"You the Sheriff?" he asked gaspingly, looking from Steele to McKee.

"The Sheriff?" Steele stared. The Scotsman said, "No. Why?"

The boy said, "Because there's a dead man back there," and gestured over his shoulder. "I was going for help. The telephone's out. Come. I'll show you."

2

Steele and McKee followed the boy on the horse up the driveway lined with trees, moving as fast as it was possible to go, slipping and sliding as they did in the heavy mud that was five or six inches deep and growing steadily deeper. It got down inside their shoes, did finally pull one of Steele's off. Broken branches littered the ground and huge round balls of tumbleweed clung to them here and there.

A sharp turn; off on the left dim lights, widely spaced, were shining pinpoints on darkness through the veils of the rain. The house at last, the boy didn't make for the front of it directly. The driveway, if you could call it that, had widened out. He led the two men through a gateway in a high adobe wall and on into a sort of huge courtyard. Low buildings flanked it here and there.

The Scotsman could see very little in the rain and the darkness but he recognized the place as a typical eighteenth-century hacienda such as Fernandez had described to him, and which was practically a fort as it had had to be then. There were very few of them left. A gated courtyard at the front on which the principal rooms opened; another at the rear where once the peons lived, carriages were housed, and the various storerooms were filled with grain and wheat and corn, bags of coffee and barrels of jerked buffalo meat, with dried fruit and herbs and strings of chili peppers hanging from the beamed ceilings.

All that was changed now. The peons and the carriages were long since gone and these buildings at the back were empty and untenanted with wide gaps between them. Light touched a broken windowpane of what looked like a chicken house, with a sagging roof. There was a general air of dilapidation, decay, about the whole place, of former grandeur now threadbare and falling slowly into ruin.

In the middle of the courtyard the boy slid from the horse, who stood docilely, head drooping. His name was Ward, Jim Ward. His voice was a Westerner's. "Over here," he said and walked left under threshing cottonwood branches and then left again toward what was evidently a kitchen door. A garbage can and an incinerator flanked it on one side. On the other, less than ten feet from the door, a man lay sprawled on his back, an arm flung out, one leg doubled under him. The man was elderly, with a dark high-nosed wrinkled face turned skyward. He wore chaps over dungarees, a heavy sweater and work boots thick with mud. His eyes were half open. They didn't move in the light of McKee's flashlight. The side of his head had been bashed in.

It was scarcely likely that anyone could have survived such a blow. That much was plain. Looking at him young Ward turned his back and retched. McKee knelt on the brick with which the courtyard was paved there and did the usual things mechanically. Feeling for a pulse he dug his fingers deeper. There was one. It was faint, and thready. He bent closer. Yes, the slightest of respirations, just barely perceptible . . . He got quickly to his feet.

"Alive," he said, dumping water out of his hat brim. "We'll have to get him inside, under cover."

It took some doing. Luckily he wasn't heavy. McKee supported the injured man's head and shoulders, Steele his legs and feet. Ward went ahead opening doors, through an entry and on into a huge kitchen. The electricity had gone with the phone. The light in the big room came from a lamp in the center of a long table and from logs flaming in a big fireplace at the far end. A woman with her back to them was standing close to the fire warming her hands. At their entrance she turned. Her hands fell to her sides. She stared at them owl-eyed—with what? Astonishment, surprise, fear?

She was middle-aged, dowdy and plain. Drab brown hair was dragged back from her face and fastened in a knot on top of her head. The steel-rimmed glasses she wore didn't help her appearance any. Passing the tip of her tongue over her lips, as though they had become suddenly dry, she kept on staring at Steele and McKee. Then her gaze dropped to the burden they were carrying, and she turned the color of ashes. She looked as though she were going to faint.

"What—who? . . ."

Her stammering agitation was extreme. Did she know the injured man? McKee wondered. There was no time for questions at that point. He said curtly, "A bedroom, the nearest," and she said, tight-lipped and short of breath, "Yes. Through there . . ." and pointed.

A minute later the badly wounded man was on a wide bed in a big gloomy room off a narrow corridor that appeared to bisect the house, at least that wing of it. His outer clothing and shoes were removed and they covered him with blankets from an old painted chest at the foot of the bed.

McKee had a flask with him. He unscrewed the top and poured brandy carefully into the flaccid mouth. It promptly ran out. He kept on patiently. Finally a little of the liquor took hold. A cough. The fellow had swallowed some of it. Not much, but the effort roused him. His closed eyes half opened and he began to mumble thickly. His voice was just barely audible against the storm outside.

"Not . . ." A pause, a muttered name, Patrick, Peter, Perez? Then, a little louder, and clearly, "Miss Mary . . ."

That was all. He stopped speaking, his eyes closed again and he lapsed back into unconsciousness. But he was still breathing. McKee had a first-aid kit in his bag in the car he had abandoned perforce. Down on one knee beside the bed he asked Ward to go and get it. Ward was eager to help. He said, "Sure thing."

"On your horse, and hurry it up, will you? Make it as fast as you can."

Eyes on the inert face of the man in the bed, high-nosed and dark-skinned, the woman who had followed them into the room unbidden said faintly, "Is he dead?" and McKee said over a shoulder, "Not quite," poured more brandy unavailingly, and got up and went over to a chair across which the man's sodden chaps and dungarees and plaid shirt were lying. The pockets of the dungarees contained a shabby wallet, a jackknife, some loose silver, a picture post card, and a large turnip watch.

The post card was addressed to Emilio Gomez, c/o Dane, Route 6, Box 430, Estancia, New Mexico and had been sent by someone called Mame. The wallet contained a five- and a one-dollar bill, a social security card and a driver's license signed with the name Emilio Gomez. The injured man was almost undoubtedly Gomez. The watch was of gold, heavily chased, a relic of at least eighty or ninety years ago. An interesting curiosity. Inside the back cover was the inscription, "William from Mary." He sprang the front cover. It had a dent in it. The watch had stopped. The hands stood at nineteen minutes of six. Almost certainly the watch had stopped when Gomez got that blow and fell to the bricks in the rear courtyard.

Looking up, he surprised the woman staring at the watch as though it had a particular meaning for her. There was a blind look in her eyes behind the glasses. Backed against the wall, she didn't answer Fernandez's description of the surviving sister, Mary Dane. McKee said pleasantly, "Mind telling me your name and who you are?"

The woman came back to attention slowly and with a conscious effort. "No, sir, of course not." She was a Mrs. Tafoya, and she had been caught by the storm on her way north from Phoenix to Albuquerque. Her car was old and not too dependable. Near the ranch her engine had begun to act up and she had turned through the El Toro gates in the hope of maybe finding a house and a telephone she could use. But the wires were down, and the lady here had been very kind and had agreed to let her stay for the night.

"Miss Dane?" McKee asked and to his surprise she said no. The lady was a Mrs. Fergusson, who had rented the hacienda from Miss Dane just recently. The story was plausible enough and it could be checked later. She seemed to be telling the truth and yet there was her queer interest in the watch, a very definite interest.

"You got here at about what time, Mrs. Tafoya?"

She thought, tucking in a strand of hair and resetting her glasses. As near as she could figure it was around half-past five. There were others already in the house, strangers, people like herself caught by the storm. McKee nodded. It was the sort of thing you read in the papers and heard over the radio, stranded travelers seeking shelter in paralyzing weather conditions. Who were the people in the house when she arrived? A man with two women, young Mr. Ward, and another man. She didn't know any of them. They were all strangers to her.

McKee had already noticed her wet hair and shoes, stout black-laced oxfords with common-sense heels. She had been out of the house recently, not long before he and

Steele had arrived. Either she was quick-witted and had seen his glance or she had nothing to be afraid of. She admitted having been outside readily enough in her awkward fumbling manner. She wanted to get her suitcase out of her car but the rain and the blackness stopped her before she had gone more than a very few feet. She had no flashlight, and she turned back. She thought someone might lend her one later . . . No, she hadn't seen the man lying on the ground a short distance away from the rear door. No, she didn't know who he was, she had never seen him before. She was sure of that? "Yes, sir, I'm sure. I was just back in the kitchen when—when you came."

She could be leveling with him; on the other hand, both her agitation when they first entered the kitchen with Gomez and her interest in the watch in his pocket had been rather extreme for a woman who was simply a stranded traveler and had no previous knowledge of the house itself or any of its occupants.

In the bed, Gomez began to snore. The snores were deep, steady. McKee swung around sharply and looked down. Coma; he didn't like it. The room was cold, dank, and the old fellow would have to be kept warm. He asked Mrs. Tafoya to get hot water and fill some bottles with it as fast as she could and she said, "Yes, sir," and went at once.

Steele was building a fire in the fireplace in the corner, there was wood and paper in a basket beside it. He at least was out of it, McKee reflected watching flames spread. It was at around five-ten that Steele had loomed up in his own headlamps on the road almost a mile from the gates and it had taken them well over three-quarters of an hour to get to the hacienda. It was a relief to have someone in the clear. There could be a killer in the house or lurking somewhere outside near it—and he was going to need help.

McKee pulled himself up short. *He* was going to need help. Standing beside the bed he gave a shrug that was half irritated, half resigned. Homicide in New York was his business but out here in the wilds of New Mexico— however at the moment it was useless to kick against the pricks. There was nothing for it but to do what he could until the weather cleared and the state and local police arrived and took over.

Ward came hurrying in, mud-splashed and drenched. McKee got the first-aid kit out of his bag. It contained adrenalin, nitroglycerine, a couple of tubes of morphine, a hypodermic, a thermometer and some bandaging gauze. Carrying it with him had become a habit. More than once on a case these things had come in handy.

Gomez was gradually sinking. There was no doubt about it. His color was worse and his pulse almost imperceptible. What was really needed was a doctor, an ambulance and a hospital. They were not immediately available, the Scotsman reflected grimly, listening to wind whirl around the house and rain that was half-sleet slam at the windows like buckshot. He gave the injured man a shot of adrenalin and stood, intently watching the weather-beaten face graven with deep lines. So did Steele and young Ward, water dripping unheeded from his khaki coat after his hurried trip to the Scotsman's damaged car.

At the end of five or six minutes a slightly easier respiration and a stronger pulse; but Gomez didn't return to consciousness. He probably had a badly fractured skull. McKee put a flaccid arm back under the blankets. All they could do until help arrived was to try and keep life in the man—if possible. The head wound was too deep to handle beyond applying a compress and a makeshift bandage. This accomplished, McKee asked Ward much the same questions he had asked Mrs. Tafoya. The young fellow frowned, trying to be accurate. He thought he had arrived at the house a little before five, he had heard a clock strike five somewhere shortly after he got in.

"Something happen to your car too, Mr. Ward?"

"*My* car?" Ward's frank blue-gray eyes opened under the brush of wiry reddish hair. "I have no car—wish I did."

"Oh? . . . Then how did you get here?"

"I walked."

"You—walked?" McKee was mildly astonished. People never walked now except in cities, and then no farther than they had to.

Ward bobbed his head. "Yes, sir—started from Rosita, where my mother lives, most four weeks ago. I had a job in a machine shop in Espanola but they were laying men off and I was the first to get the sack because I was the youngest and not married or nothing. My right lung isn't too good and I figured I could get work in Albuquerque, they say it's growing like blazes, or even farther down, maybe Phoenix. I did get a job in Albuquerque but it was only for ten days. So I decided to keep going. I left there early this morning. The hills are pretty steep and the wind was bad so I couldn't make much time. Anyhow, I was dead beat when I got this far and that woman, Mrs. Fergusson, allowed I could stay the night kind of—well, she didn't like it much."

"There were other people here when you arrived?"

Ward said sure, that there was a swell car, a big Rolls, and a couple of others parked near the house. He was pretty dirty and he had gone around to the back. If Gomez was there then, he didn't see him. The electricity was still on and he made straight for the kitchen door. "I guess," he said with a shy smile, "when I come in Mrs. Fergusson decided one more wouldn't hurt, and besides, that Mrs. Tafoya put in a good word for me."

The two women were the only ones he had seen. After he got in, he was covered with mud, he had spent quite a while getting himself cleaned up in a kind of scullery off the kitchen. He looked down ruefully at his high-laced boots freshly daubed to the knees.

The Scotsman considered. The attack on Gomez had

been made at nineteen minutes of six. He and Steele had
run into Ward galloping down the driveway at better than
half-past, over three-quarters of an hour later. He asked
Ward at what time and how he had discovered Gomez in
the rear courtyard.

As to when, Ward couldn't say exactly, he had no
watch. As to how he had come on him, he had gone outside
for wood for the kitchen fire, he had had a glimpse of a
long stack of it at the far side of the courtyard when he
first came into the hacienda. No, no one had suggested that
he go get the wood but the supply in the kitchen was low—
"and I thought I'd kind of make myself useful, do what I
could to help." Blundering around in the darkness he had
almost fallen over what he had decided was a dead man.
That was when he had got the horse from the corral on
his own and ridden off for help.

"Why didn't you let the people here know—tell Mrs.
Fergusson, anyhow?"

"I tried to, sir," Ward eaid earnestly, "I did try. I
ran inside—but there was no one in the kitchen and the
lights were gone by then and the phone was out, too. I
guess, with the darkness and this house and all"—he waved
a hand—"I—I got scared. It was—kind of spooky. I knew
there were horses, the corral's just over from the back
gateway, and there were a couple of halters on a post, and
on my map there's a town three miles or so to the south
where I thought maybe there'd be a sheriff or someone like
that . . ."

McKee studied him thoughtfully. He was a plain
freckle-faced lad with brownish-red hair in a crew cut
and good features, intelligent enough but clearly unnerved
by what had happened. Like Mrs. Tafoya, he could be
telling the truth. He could also have been escaping the
scene of a crime in a hurry . . . It was much too early
to come to a decision about either one of them. There were
others to be interviewed, and a lot of work to be done

before they could get anywhere. He was starting to dismiss Ward when he broke off abruptly.

Out of the corner of his eye he saw the heavy iron latch of the door lift and the door begin to open. Before he got around the end of the bed the door had closed again, soundlessly. The room was big. By the time he reached the door and opened it, there was no one in the narrow corridor outside, and nothing but blackness. Other doors right and left, plenty of bolt holes into one of which someone might have slipped, must have, because the latch didn't lift of itself.

McKee gave a mental shrug, turned back, let Ward go and, alone with Steele, asked him if he'd mind staying with Gomez while he talked to the other people in the house. "Someone just tried to get in here . . ."

Steele was beyond surprise. Anything was possible in this place. Brows up he nodded at the still figure in the bed. "You mean—to finish the job, Inspector?"

McKee had already told Steele who he was. "Could be," he agreed. "Looks rather like it from the way whoever it was took off when he, or she, found we were in here."

"Then it couldn't have been that Mrs. Tafoya," Steele argued. "She knows we're here, so it must have been one of the others. Narrows it down a bit."

"Yes." The oil lamp on a marble-topped stand in the corner was smoking. McKee lowered the flame slightly. At that point Mrs. Tafoya tapped softly and entered the room with her awkward round-shouldered gait. Her arms were loaded with bottles wrapped in toweling. "The hot water," she said, "I think it's just about right." She pushed aside the table with the first-aid kit on it and began inserting the bottles under the blankets with which Gomez was covered to the chin. She did it neatly and skillfully, with no trace of her former nervousness. Gomez might have been a log of wood for all the emotion she showed.

Straightening up, she said to McKee in her drab voice,

"Anything else I can do, sir? I know about sick people, how to take temperatures and feed them, I used to have a job helping in a hospital." The Scotsman thanked her, said he didn't believe there was anything more she could do at the moment, and she went.

Leaning against the wall, hands in his pockets, Steele watched her go curiously. He was frowning. "You know," he said thoughtfully when the door had closed behind her, "it's odd, but I have a feeling that I've seen that woman somewhere before—yes, I'm pretty sure of it, but it wasn't out here in these parts, this is my first trip to the Southwest."

Attempted murder by someone in or near the house; the slightest shred of knowledge about any of these people now in it was important. "Any idea of when or where you saw her?" McKee asked. But Steele couldn't remember. There were fragments, though.

"A slop pail—and a scrubbing brush—down on her knees. That's right . . ." But try as he would it was all he could manage to fish up.

A pail and a scrubbing brush—the woman looked as though she might have been a servant at one time. "Don't press and it may come," McKee said.

He had been examining the room at intervals and he decided that it had almost certainly been Veronica Dane's. The initial V was embroidered on the faded satin spread that had been thrown back. It was an austere chamber the late Veronica had inhabited, as far as comfort went.

He looked around at the beamed ceiling, the heavy *vigas* and whitewashed walls, the three straight hand-hewn chairs with worn rawhide seats, a few small, fine but almost threadbare Navajo rugs on the floor, the bed itself, a cheap washstand with basin and pitcher, a handsome painted chest, and a ponderous, highly carved desk of what looked like ebony.

These last were pieces from other lands and very old. They had probably been transported by an early Dane ancestor from Mexico City by way of Chihuahua more than a century and a half ago. According to Fernandez, Veronica Dane had an almost fanatical family feeling and as far as possible she had kept everything as it was in her grandfather's time. Ancestor worship, an immersion in the past—because the present had failed her? Could be . . .

Why dwell on her? She was dead and in her grave. Perhaps it was because she had stamped her personality on the room, seemed in an odd way to pervade it as though she were still alive. McKee roused himself, and looked at Gomez. There was no change. If only the man could speak . . . The four words he had managed to get out were meaningless. "Not—" then a man's name, Peter or Perez or Patrick, then "Miss Mary . . ." A blast of wind struck furiously at the windows and the oil lamp started to smoke a little. He adjusted the wick again. "I want to talk to the others here but I won't be long," he said to Steele, and picked up his flashlight.

He needed it. The hall was in complete darkness. He went along it to the kitchen. There was light enough there, from a big oil lamp on the table in the center of the huge old room. Whitewashed walls, discolored with smoke in places, the great fireplace had formerly been used for cooking; implements of black iron hung on either side. Mrs. Tafoya was filling a kettle at the soapstone sink. Drawing herself together she swung around like a startled animal at McKee's entrance, relaxed when she saw who it was.

He wondered who she had expected to see, and feared. There had been what looked remarkably like fright in her wheeling crouch . . . It could be simply nerves on her part, or perhaps his own imagination working overtime. Everyone and everything in the place seemed faintly dubious, distorted, subtly out of shape. Perhaps, he grinned inwardly, it was his Scots blood, and this old hacienda lifted bodily out of another century was infecting him. He turned almost as sharply as Mrs. Tafoya when a door on the far side of the room was pushed open and a woman came in. The woman was Mrs. Fergusson, who had rented El Toro from Mary Dane.

Mrs. Fergusson had an assured carriage and was good-looking in a hard brassy way. Staring at McKee she pulled up short in astonishment.

"Who are *you?*"

The demand was abrupt. There was exasperation in her stare. Under the circumstances it was natural enough. You don't ordinarily expect to find perfect strangers making themselves at home in your kitchen. McKee gave her his name without his title and explained his and Steele's predicament, the smash-up of their cars on the road not too far from the driveway, and their discovery of the name over the gateposts. A friend of his back East was an old and close friend of the Dane family. "He asked me to stop by while I was out here if I got the chance—which I didn't expect to be able to do. It was—more or less thrust on me." He smiled pleasantly.

Mrs. Fergusson didn't smile. "And this man with you?"

McKee said he was a Mr. Steele, a writer from New York on a tour of the Southwest, and told her about the meeting with Ward and finding Gomez lying on the ground and badly wounded in the courtyard beyond the kitchen door.

Some of the antagonism, not all, went out of her. She exclaimed that she had never seen Emilio Gomez but knew who he was.

Almost a full hour had passed since he and Steele had carried Gomez into the house. McKee apologized for having come into the hacienda without permission but there was nothing else to be done and she wasn't around.

Mrs. Fergusson didn't soften. The hard suspicion in her remained constant. She said that Emilio Gomez was, or rather had been, the Danes' yardman, and he was to have come for the stock that was still there, two horses and some chickens and some other animals, late that afternoon. He hadn't turned up, but, she shrugged, she had thought nothing of it, laid it to the storm.

McKee nodded. "I can see that." Gomez an old servant of the Danes. Very interesting. Someone in or near the house had given him that blow which would have been instantly lethal except for a thick skull . . . He and Steele had made a certain amount of noise tramping in with the unconscious man. Mrs. Fergusson explained her nonappearance by saying she had been taking a nap. With the long day, her first full one there, and a lot of strangers tramping in out of nowhere she was pretty tired . . .

She didn't look like a woman who had been asleep, on the contrary she was very much alive and alert—and not in a good temper. Perhaps it was habitual. McKee asked whether she could recall at what time she had gone to her room.

She couldn't say exactly, only that it was after the last of them, young Ward, had come—"Except you and your friend."

Mrs. Tafoya was the first, then a man and two women had appeared, and then another man. No, she didn't know where they were now, any of them, probably in the rooms they had appropriated without a by-your-leave. She crossed the room and began to make coffee, banging pots around. Luckily the stove, almost the only modern fitting in the kitchen, was fed by bottle gas. She only hoped the gas wouldn't give out, but—another shrug—they'd all be gone by morning with the help of God.

An odd woman. No compassion, not showing anyhow. She appeared to have no curiosity whatever about who had attacked Gomez, nor was she much concerned about him. She merely said curtly that El Toro was no place for him. "He ought to be in the hospital, that's where he ought to be." McKee agreed emphatically and left the kitchen.

Beyond it was a serving pantry fitted with glass-fronted cabinets. There was a second swing door at the far end that evidently led to the dining room. It had a round unglassed hole in it the size of a small plate. The pantry was dark. There was light beyond the hole. McKee bent and looked through it.

The light came from a lamp on a long carved refectory table that would have seated twelve people comfortably. In the outside wall to the left of the table there were two windows. A woman was standing at one of the windows in profile to him. She had a hat on and also her coat. The coat was mink and a handsome one. McKee stared. He had seen the woman early that morning, in the White Queen Hotel in Denver.

She had seemed ill and she was leaving the lobby hastily between a man and a girl. McKee had been standing within a yard of them as they passed. The reason he had noticed the trio was because the man supporting the mink-coated woman was Henry Hilliard, head of the investment house of Jones, Silver and Hilliard in New York, and a well-known figure in Wall Street.

The woman was tall and handsome in a lush way, soft-looking and used to luxury and pampering. Hilliard was married and McKee had concluded she was his wife. As the trio went through the hotel lobby Hilliard was saying something about the weather, that it didn't look promising, and his wife had cut him short almost hysterically. "No, Henry, no. I *won't* stay here. I tell you I'll be all right as soon as I get into the air and we get started . . ." Driving south the Hilliard party had evidently been caught here by the storm as he had himself. Certainly a varied kettle of fish had turned up at the El Toro ranch somewhere in the wilderness of the Sandias . . .

In the room beyond, Mrs. Hilliard was leaning forward

peering through the wet black pane. Her hands were cupped around her eyes. There was an odd intensity in her stance. What was she looking at, trying to see in the darkness and the rain? About to push the door open, the Scotsman remained where he was. A girl's voice said, "Rita," and the woman at the window dropped her hands and turned quickly.

"What were you staring out at?" the girl asked and Rita Hilliard said carelessly and with a languid composure she hadn't exhibited a moment before, "To see if it's still raining hard, and whether perhaps we couldn't get on, get out of this place . . . I don't *like* this beastly mausoleum, Jill, it absolutely gives me the creeps. And these awful people . . ."

The girl retorted, "Well, you can give up the idea of leaving tonight, Rita—Henry says it's absolutely impossible—so you might as well take off your hat and coat and stay a while."

"I suppose so," the ample white and gold beauty sighed, and passed out of view. McKee pushed the door open.

Mrs. Hilliard and the girl had gone through a wide archway into a spacious room at the right. It could only be called a drawing room. Whitewashed walls had a six-feet dado of faded pinkish cloth running around them. Carved corbels supported the *viga* ceiling, an old-fashioned grand piano the size of a houseboat in shadow; the furniture in fire and candlelight was stiff, stately. Flames danced up from logs piled in the adobe fireplace at the far end but in spite of the fire the air had a bite to it.

Thirty feet out in front Mrs. Hilliard was seating herself on a faded satin sofa, huddled in her furs. The girl stood close to the fire, one slender arched foot on the raised hearthstone, her hands in the pockets of a red wool dress. She was tallish, five feet five or six, and slight, with pale gold hair drawn back from a narrow face that was interesting rather than pretty, a striking, provocative face. As McKee advanced a door behind the fireplace at the far end opened and Henry Hilliard walked in.

He was considerably younger than his wife, a strong vigorous man in his late thirties, who knew what he was doing and precisely where he was bound for. He carried himself with an air of quiet authority, the authority of sureness. Joining the girl at the fire he slid an arm around her shoulders. His daughter? But she was much too old for that.

"Aren't you cold, dear, with no coat on?" he asked solicitously.

"No," the girl said, "I'm not cold particularly, but I'll tell you what I am, I'm starving." As she spoke she moved a little and Hilliard dropped his arm. "Starving, are you? We'll have to do something about that. It won't be difficult. There'll be plenty of food here if I know my El Toro . . ." Turning he caught sight of the Scotsman coming in from the dining room and came to a standstill, frowning.

He and McKee had met casually at two or three civic functions in New York. He's trying to place me, McKee thought, strolling forward slowly, and hoped he wouldn't. Hilliard did.

"*Inspector*," he exclaimed after a second, his face clearing. "Well, well, this is a surprise . . . What are *you* doing out here in this part of the world? . . . Caught by the storm like ourselves, I suppose?" He shook hands cordially, and introduced the two women. McKee listened with half an ear. Someone had entered, and left, the dining room while Hilliard was speaking . . . He wondered who it was.

"Mrs. Mole," Hilliard was waving at the large beauty on the sofa, "and this," he put a hand on the girl's arm, "is my fiancée, Miss Sheppard."

Bowing to the girl, McKee was aware of a feeling of

slight shock. It was not a discrepancy of age, that wasn't too great. Miss Sheppard was in her mid-twenties. It was the girl herself. There was something mutinous in her, almost petulant, and her manner was not that of a happily engaged young woman. She looked rather a handful . . . Hilliard had been married, his first wife must have died . . .

McKee told all three of them what had happened, succinctly. A man, struck down outside the back door a short time earlier, and in all probability fatally wounded.

On the sofa Mrs. Mole stared at him, white-faced. She gave a cry and fell back limply against the cushions, pressing a handkerchief to her lips. "Oh dear, oh dear, I *knew* it. This place . . . We shouldn't have stopped, we should have gone on." The girl said nothing, simply looked at him, her lashes wide. She wasn't the jittery type. Not at all. Hilliard was grave.

"Good heavens . . . Who is the fellow who was hurt, Inspector? Do you know? Have you been able to find out?"

McKee said, "Yes, Mr. Hilliard, his name is Gomez, Emilio Gomez, and according to Mrs. Fergusson, the tenant here, he used to work for the Danes, as a yard and handyman, I believe."

"*Emilio* . . . God," Hilliard exclaimed, taking out a handkerchief and wiping his forehead. He was shocked and moved. He said he had been born and brought up on a ranch some fifteen miles or so south of El Toro and he had known both the Danes and Emilio well for many years. His own father and mother still lived on their ranch part of the year at least. His father was ill. He and his fiancée and her sister, Mrs. Mole, had been on the way down to see him when they were stopped by the storm. They had already passed El Toro but had had to turn back. According to the radio in his car the bridge over a tributary of the Rio Grande they had to cross was out and they could go no farther east.

Hilliard and his party had reached the hacienda at

shortly before five o'clock. He knew Veronica Dane was dead, he had heard the news from his people while he was in New York, but he had expected to find Mary Dane at the hacienda, it was almost impossible to imagine Mary anywhere else, she had lived here all her life. But Mary wasn't here. It seemed she had rented the place. It was the tenant, a Mrs. Fergusson, who had opened the door to them. Emilio wasn't anywhere in evidence. The only people they themselves had seen were a woman named Sanchez or something like that. "Tafoya," McKee said, and Hilliard nodded. "Yes, that was it. Common name in New Mexico. There's also a young fellow named Ward. Both of them, like ourselves, were on their way somewhere else, and—"

"Orphans of the storm," Miss Sheppard suggested, lighting a cigarette and dropping the match carelessly to the broad soapstone hearth. Hilliard stooped and picked it up absently and tossed it into the fire. "Yes, that's right."

All his movements were easy. He was in excellent physical trim. He smiled at the girl. It was obvious that he was deeply in love. When he smiled he had a great deal of charm. He turned back to McKee. "And I believe there's another older man here, a salesman. I didn't get his name or see him but Mrs. Fergusson—" He broke off.

Mrs. Mole had been lying back on the brocaded sofa that had once been green and gold, looking, around the edges of disinterest, both bored and cross. The sofa faced the front of the house. All at once she sat up sharply. She was staring at one of the windows. Her mouth was a little open and there was a ring of pallor around it.

McKee swung. So did the others. A shadow on shadows beyond the rain-drenched panes? Something out there? Someone looking in? The Scotsman was across the rug and at the door in half a dozen strides. He pulled the door open. Hilliard was at his heels.

Outside rain and blackness and wind and tumult caught at them. The window through which Mrs. Mole had stared was twenty feet or so to the right. The two men ducked under an untrimmed fruit tree of some sort and out onto a lawn dotted with trees and clumps of bushes. There was no one near the windows.

McKee switched his light downward, moved it this way and that—and held it still. No, there was no one there now, but there had been someone there. The grass wouldn't take footprints—it was too thick, a heavy mat—but low shrubbery under the windows showed fresh breaks in their intertwined boughs that gleamed white in the light . . .

McKee straightened, pushed rain out of his eyes and looked around. But it was obvious that further search out there would be utterly useless, a waste of time. Whoever had wanted to see into the lighted living room, see what was going on, had taken to his heels when the front door opened. The Scotsman and Hilliard went back inside, turned their coat collars down and dried their faces with handkerchiefs.

Mrs. Mole was talking to her young sister. She had partially recovered her composure but she was still fearful. There was a faintly hysterical note in her voice. "I *did* think I saw something move . . . Maybe it *was* just my nerves, I don't know . . . Or it could have been an animal, a cow or a horse . . . Oh, this terrible place."

In the Scotsman's opinion it was neither her nerves nor an animal. The bushes were cacti, and a horse or cow would have steered clear at the first hint of them.

Mrs. Mole looked at the two men, her mouth bunched together as though she were afraid of a blow. Hilliard said calmly, "Relax, Rita, take it easy. No one out there, not now, at any rate. But anyhow I think we ought to lock up, Inspector, just in case, to be on the safe side."

"Yes."

The girl's eyes were brilliant between rims of dark lash and there was a rose flush on her cheeks. Excitement evidently stimulated her . . . "Perhaps," she suggested, put-

ting a match to a fresh cigarette, "you may be locking whoever attacked that man, that poor Mr. Gomez, into the
house and not out."

It was McKee's own thought. The people there now
could be dealt with, up to a point. Certainly there was no
need of any addition to the present collection. He suggested
that Hilliard take the first floor. "I'll take upstairs. Then I
want to have a word with that salesman and see if he has any
information to give us."

"Right." Hilliard walked off briskly and McKee
mounted the stairs. The fall of the house of Usher, he
thought as he went. Even with daylight and the sun
shining, the hacienda would still be big and gloomy and
depressing. Now with only the beam of his light it was
something out of a horror movie. Darkness before him,
darkness closing in behind. Glimpses of faded tapestries,
old portraits, closed doors pulled into being and relapsing
back into nothingness. He began at the north end of the
long corridor that bisected the house.

One empty room after another, three of them in
succession, old furniture, some of it good, a smell of dust
and cobwebs and mice. Then an occupied room. He
opened the door, and came to a halt just over the threshold.

There was a man peacefully asleep in the high painted
bed. He was all but invisible under the covers. Only the
top of his sandy-haired head showed. He was snoring
gently. The light didn't wake him. He didn't stir. He must
be the salesman Hilliard had mentioned. An open suitcase
lay on top of a carved chest, a shaving kit spread out beside
it. The suitcase held a pair of red and white striped pajamas,
a pair of shorts, two pairs of socks, a tie and a blue bathrobe. The fellow's suit jacket was draped over a chair and
a pair of muddy shoes were on the floor near the bed.
McKee examined the coat, a wary eye on the bed. A bunch
of keys in the right hand pocket, in the breast pocket two

brochures on synthetic whalebone and a filled cigar case —nothing informative.

McKee was about to rouse the man when a rumpus broke out somewhere below and he left the room fast. The front doorbell rang loudly, and went on ringing. Someone was pounding on it and shouting distantly. McKee made for the staircase, paused at the head of it. The two leaves of the front door were glass, small-paned and covered with carefully mended lace panels. As he started down, one of the panes smashed and a hand came through the jagged hole and twisted the latch. The door was flung open. Rain and wind came in with it, making the lamp on the piano shoot up and down smokily. The others were there by that time: Mrs. Mole, Jill Sheppard and Hilliard near the ineffectual fire, Mrs. Fergusson, Mrs. Tafoya and young Ward in the dining-room archway.

The man who had entered the room by such drastic means slammed the door unceremoniously shut behind him. He was tall and lean, wore a windbreaker, dungarees and boots. Dashing wetness out of his eyes he looked around. "Where is she?" he demanded eagerly in a loud voice. "Did she make it? Is she here?"

Someone said, "Is *who* here?" and the stranger said, "Miss Mary, Mary Dane."

3

The new arrival was a man named Bill Speaker, the rancher who had driven Mary Dane away from the hacienda the morning before. He knew Hilliard and Hilliard knew him. When the rancher had collected himself the two men shook hands, and Speaker asked about Mr. Hilliard senior. "Heard your father wasn't feeling well. Fine gentleman. Stopped in sometimes on my way south to get horses." After that Hilliard introduced the two nearest women and McKee. Speaker explained the urgency of his visit.

His ranch, his wife's and his, was four miles to the north and Mary was going to stay with them there for a month or so until she looked about her and decided what she was going to do. Mary had left the Speaker ranch at around four o'clock that afternoon, unexpectedly. At the time she went Speaker was out rounding up some sheep that had strayed and his wife, Edith, was in the hen house feeding the chickens. When Edith got in, and she hadn't been outside much over twenty minutes, Mary was gone. But there was a note from her propped against the sugar bowl in the kitchen.

Mary said she had forgotten something important and was going back to El Toro to get it, and that she wouldn't be long. She had taken the old piebald mare, Polo, and had ridden over, or that had been her intention at least. Neither of the Speakers was too worried at first, Mary knew the countryside like the palm of her hand. But after a while, when darkness began to come on and the storm steadily worsened, they began to get really anxious. The wind was blowing a gale and a half and the rain was mixed with sleet.

"We tried to phone thinking that she might be going to stay the night here at El Toro," Speaker said, "but the line was dead." Finally at his wife's insistence, he had driven over in the pick-up truck, and tough going it was.

"She didn't get here?" he asked again, his forehead corrugating.

By then Mrs. Tafoya and Ward had returned to the kitchen. Mrs. Fergusson remained, arms folded, an alert and watchful spectator without expression.

"No," she said decisively. "Other people came, but not Miss Dane. The last I saw of her was yesterday morning."

Speaker gave his head a shake. He didn't like it at all. Mary might have had an accident riding across country, which was what she had probably done. She might have been hit by a falling tree or Polo might have put her foot into a pothole and broken a leg and thrown her. Any number of things might have happened.

Obviously a search at night in this weather, over a considerable stretch of territory, would be hopeless and the storm showed no sign of letting up. He said he'd have to get back home while he could and start to look for her at the first crack of dawn.

Hilliard was also concerned about Mary Dane, whom he had known since he was a boy. Mrs. Fergusson's concern appeared to be solely for the broken pane of glass in the front door. Rain was driving through the jagged hole and puddling the floor. "What about that?" She pointed. "Who's going to fix that?"

The rancher looked at her briefly and grinned. He said he'd fix it in a few minutes, with a piece of wood from the stables. She said curtly, "The sooner the better," and walked away.

The rancher was anxious to be off. "But first I'd better attend to that damn door."

When he went out to the stables for wood and a hammer and nails McKee went with him. He wanted a word with Speaker alone. But it was impossible to talk in the open. The din was terrific and the gale had increased in force. They had to fight their way across a black inferno of howling wind and water, heads down. Inside the barn under cover, when he got his breath, McKee told the rancher about the attack on Emilio earlier in the evening. Speaker was rummaging through a pile of miscellaneous bits and pieces of wood stacked in a corner. He reared himself and faced around in amazement.

"*Emilio?* Someone tried to kill *Emilio?*" He was incredulous. "But why? What for?"

McKee said, "I was hoping you might be able to tell me, Mr. Speaker."

But the rancher had no light to shed. He was completely baffled, couldn't understand it, kept shaking a puzzled head. As far as he knew Emilio hadn't an enemy in the world and owned nothing of any value, except the old gentleman's, Mary's father's, gold watch; it was the pride of his life. He had been with the Danes more than twenty years and Charles Dane had left it to him in his will.

Recalling Fernandez's remark about Veronica in the Commissioner's office almost three thousand miles to the Northeast, "I always thought someone would kill her," McKee asked a few questions about the family.

Speaker shrugged. "I don't know that I can tell you

very much." He said that in his time he had only known the two sisters. Veronica was the big chief, the boss . . . She walked all over her younger sister, but that was her nature. She was born that way, imperious, and probably couldn't help it. "She was all right, I guess." Popular in the neighborhood? Decidedly not. An autocrat from the word go, and proud as Lucifer.

"She could slay you with a look if you happened to get on the wrong side of her. She couldn't stand opposition of any kind." He personally had given her a wide berth. If she had been hard with people she had been wonderful with animals. He spoke of the dog Spot and his disappearance the day she died and the behavior of her stallion ever since. Mary Dane had told him about it when he drove over for her yesterday. She was another kettle of fish altogether. Everyone was fond of her. She was always kind and would do anything for anyone she could.

"She never complained about Veronica?"

"She never complained about anything."

McKee toed wisps of hay, hands in his pockets. Two women living out here alone together in the wilds, day after day, month after month, year in year out, with very little or no diversion; Veronica the dominating older one, Mary the placator, the yielder . . . The turn of the worm? . . . Perhaps. It could be. After Veronica's sudden death there was for instance the immediate putting of the house on the market by Mary and her desire to get away from El Toro as fast as she could . . . And then, he thought of Emilio Gomez, and Gomez's murmured words, the only words the stricken yardman had managed to get out: "Not Peter"— or Patrick or Perez—". . . Miss Mary."

Mary Dane had announced her intention of coming over here to El Toro late that afternoon for something she'd forgotten. She hadn't reached the ranch. But Emilio had been struck down by a would-be killer . . . The Scotsman eyed the flame of the lantern Speaker had lit. That line of reasoning wouldn't wash. If Gomez had known something incriminating to Mary Dane where Veronica's death was concerned, she wouldn't wait for almost three weeks to put him out of business, silence him permanently. Unless . . . Gomez might only have shown his hand that day—which would mean that Mary had reached El Toro.

And Mary had.

Bill Speaker had gone into the tackroom off on the right to get some small nails he wanted, whistling softly through his teeth. The Scotsman listened absently. The sound was thin against the creaking of timbers, the drive of the wind. All at once the whistling stopped and Speaker gave a shout. "Hi—Inspector."

McKee joined him, side-stepping a harrow. Saddles and bridles and shining bits beginning to be speckled with rust hung around the tackroom walls on pegs. There was a battered armchair in a corner; a long work bench with an assortment of tools, and odds and ends scattered over it, ran along one wall. Speaker was pointing. What he pointed at was a pair of worn tan leather gauntlets lying in shadow half under an old rubber boot.

The gauntlets were Mary Dane's. Speaker said so positively. Mary had been wearing them when she drove away with him from the ranch yesterday morning. The leather of the gauntlets was wet. Yes, Mary had reached the ranch . . . If she had left the Speakers' at four she could have been there by five and waited here in the barn for Gomez to appear. There was no other evidence of her in the tackroom, or the barn, or the stables proper. McKee and Speaker made a hasty tour. Bales of hay, a huge mound of oats, a smell of ammonia and manure and grain, and opening out of the barn in the stable itself a half dozen stalls. There was a horse in one of the stalls. It was Veronica Dane's stallion, Carlo.

The stallion reared violently in the sudden light of McKee's torch. Eyes shining redly, he brought all four feet down, stamped hard on the flooring and kicked out wickedly with his hind legs. McKee kept his distance. "Savage-looking brute." Speaker nodded. "He's in a state all right. I wouldn't want to handle him myself until he calms down. He's going to need a lot of gentling."

Carlo was the only horse in the stables. The piebald, Polo, that Mary Dane had ridden over to El Toro wasn't there. The black horse Ward had been riding when they intercepted him in the driveway must be still in the rear courtyard.

Mary might, as Speaker suggested, have come in here to put Polo under cover in one of the stalls while she did what she had come back to El Toro to do. Then what? An advance on the house itself? An encounter with Emilio Gomez in the courtyard, and that blow meant to kill, after which she had ridden away without being seen by anyone? . . . Find Mary and get the truth out of her was the answer. McKee had an idea it was going to be a difficult job. She knew the country well and she had had a three hours' start . . . Also there were other possibilities.

He said nothing of this to Speaker. In any case, he reminded himself irascibly again, it was not his affair. Gomez's death, if he did die, was the business of the New Mexico police. Sooner or later day would come and the storm would be over and communications restored and the roads open. Meanwhile his was just a holding operation for the night.

Speaker was eyeing the stallion with a frown. "Wonder why he's in this stall instead of in his own loose box? Oh well, finicky fellow, likes his own way. Carlo, easy, boy, easy." He tried in vain to soothe the stallion. It was impossible. McKee collected Mary's gauntlets from the bench in the tackroom and the two men left the barn and started back to the hacienda. Again it was a battle. If anything, the rain was coming down harder than ever in almost solid sheets and the wind had stepped up its fury. As they fought their way to the house, making for the front door which was nearest, McKee pulled up short. The light in the late Veronica Dane's room, the room where the badly injured Gomez lay, watched over by Steele, was on when they left the hacienda half an hour ago. Now the light was out. McKee began to run.

The front door was locked. The rancher thrust a hand through the broken pane just as he had done before and lifted the latch. There was no one in the long living room when they dashed through it at top speed and on into the dark corridor beyond. McKee rapped sharply on the door halfway along its length. At first there was no answer. "Steele," he called urgently, "Steele," and rapped again more loudly. Finally there was movement beyond the heavy panels. It was slow, fumbling. After another couple of seconds Steele opened the door. He blinked in the light of McKee's flashlight, rubbed his eyes. The room behind him was in darkness. Steele was still half asleep. He said groggily, "I must have dozed off . . ."

The Scotsman was already past him and across to the wide bed. Speaker followed him and stared down.

"It's Emilio all right," he said pityingly. "What a shame. Poor old guy, looks as though he's done for . . ."

Gomez was breathing at any rate. Under the blanket his chest rose and fell. McKee said, not believing his own words, "I don't know, you can't tell, he may have a chance," and wiped sweat from his forehead in spite of the chill in the air. At least Gomez was alive. No attempt had apparently been made on him and the room was undisturbed—except that the lamp was out. The Scotsman examined it.

The lamp had been blown out. And not by the wind. There was very little draft. The windows were all locked, and the wick was high. The door was also locked until Steele had opened it to let them in. Yet someone had been in there . . . Steele hadn't extinguished the lamp. He said so.

"Of course I didn't. It was on when I closed my eyes for just a minute to rest them . . . I had no intention of going to sleep, but obviously I must have conked off . . .

You think that while I was asleep there was someone in here, Inspector?"

"Yes, and not long ago." McKee relit the lamp. "This chimney's still hot."

"But I don't see—how *could* anyone get in?" Steele was bewildered.

It was Speaker who supplied the answer to his question. "There is a way . . . Come over here, Inspector, and I'll show you."

He crossed the floor toward the far wall. A tapestry hung there behind the heavy desk. The rancher shoved the desk out of the way with a lean hip, it moved easily enough on the tiled floor. He lifted the tapestry, and pulled it to one side. There was a small door in back of it. This door was unlocked. It opened on a small whitewashed room, a cubicle not more than seven or eight feet square. There were no windows. The only furniture it contained was a prie-dieu, its faded cushioning in tatters, placed below a triptych that enclosed three dark paintings, a crucifixion, a Madonna and child, and the flight into Egypt. A narrow ladder-like iron staircase rose in the opposite corner.

Speaker remained with the unconscious Gomez while McKee and Steele mounted the steep treads. They emerged in a lumber room above full of discarded stuff, pictures in stacks, broken chairs, a table minus a leg and old trunks with rounded tops stacked against the walls. There were windows there, three of them. They were small. There was also a skylight near the massive chimney that rose in the middle. The lumber room could have been entered through the skylight, and in all probability there was a door at the far end.

McKee started in search of it, and stood still listening. A faint click of metal somewhere out in front? It was. The sound was very slight against the steady drumming of rain on the roof overhead. It wasn't repeated. The Scotsman knew what it was. It was the sound of a latch being dropped softly into place. He moved on fast, but by the time he reached the far door and got it open the corridor outside was dark and empty. Nothing moved along its length. Light seeping up from the floor below was a faint blur at the top of the staircase more than forty feet away. There was no one silhouetted against it.

But there were other doors right and left, giving on rooms into which someone could have silently retreated. These doors were all closed. It was the experience of a few hours ago repeated over again. Hilliard, McKee knew, was in this part of the house, and Mrs. Mole, and Jill Sheppard. In addition to the bedrooms there were two other staircases beside the main one down which someone could have vanished. One led to the kitchen at the southern end of the house and there was another at the northern end, off to the left.

McKee looked at the bedroom doors speculatively but —dilly-dilly, come out and be killed—even if he managed to locate someone up here, he, or she, was certainly not going to admit having been in the lumber room a minute earlier. He turned slowly back.

Steele had already mounted to the skylight, by setbacks in the bricks of the chimney. Descending as the Scotsman came toward him, and dusting his hands, he said the skylight could be lifted. It was heavy, its own weight held it down, but there didn't appear to be any other fastenings.

McKee nodded. You could take your choice. Veronica Dane's room, the room in which the yardman lay, could have been entered via the roof by some agile climber from outside the hacienda. To negotiate a parallel cottonwood branch and drop down on it would have been no trick at all. Or it could have been done by someone already in the house, Mrs. Fergusson or one of the impromptu and oddly assorted guests who had sought shelter at El Toro for the night. The question of why anyone had made that surreptitious entry was something else again . . .

The two men returned to the bedroom below by the

way they had come. Speaker was doing patrol duty restlessly up and down the floor. There was nothing more he
could do here and he was concerned about the continuing
storm and anxious to get off. His wife would be worried
about him.

The rain showed no sign of letting up. It was a dull
monotonous obligato, now louder, now softer, but going on
steadily. There was something inexorable about it, as though
it would never stop. Speaker said that if it kept on like that
till morning there'd be floods perhaps, and more roads
washed out and trees down. He said that Edith would probably be half frantic by this time. Another reason for his
wanting to get home was that when he did he might find
Mary Dane there, safe and sound. Speaker was hopeful
about it. In any case he said that if Mary was still missing
when morning came, a search for her would be mounted and
the state police notified in some fashion or other. She had
to be located. It was possible that she had taken refuge in
one of the caves in the cliffs on higher ground. There were
plenty of them.

Before he left the room the Scotsman asked him if there
were any pictures of Mary Dane in the house and the
rancher thought for a moment and said yes. There were a
lot of photographs on the wall of the corridor outside, near
the far end of it over some bookcases. "I'll just fix that
broken pane and then be on my way." He waved a hand
and closed the door behind him.

McKee began to examine the room they were in more
closely. He started with the desk. Inside the heavy dropleaf
a series of small drawers and pigeonholes lined the back
of it. It was at once evident that whoever had entered the
room while Steele was asleep had searched the desk in a
hurry. The drawers had been pulled out and pushed back
crookedly. A couple of them were half open. He had given
the inside of it a casual glance earlier and it was in no such
condition then. It was impossible to say what, if anything,

had been taken. It held very little; a couple of old leather-bound books in Spanish, a few inconsequential papers in the pigeonholes, half a dozen bills stamped paid, for oil, for grain, for electricity and the telephone. There was a grocery list with the items checked off, an advertisement for a new pump and an empty envelope addressed to Miss Veronica Dane at El Toro.

McKee turned it over. The return address on the back said Mrs. Robert Adams, 1058 Canyon Road, Santa Fe, New Mexico. The paper was expensive. Veronica Dane had probably kept the envelope because of the return address, which was engraved. The searcher couldn't have been looking for it or it would have been removed. However, nothing was too small as a possible pointer and it might come in handy later when they knew more. He pocketed it carefully.

The ransacking of the desk might be only part of what the intruder stepping silently into the room had come here to do . . . Steele heavily asleep in a chair near the fire in the dim light, an attack on Gomez might have been the next step if he and Speaker hadn't arrived when they did.

At his elbow Steele was curious and interested. He said, "Anything?" and McKee said, "Not now, but there may be fingerprints," and closed the desk. "I'm going to try to find out what all these people here have been doing for the last three-quarters of an hour or so, that is—if I can. I won't be long. You don't mind staying on here for a short time?"

Steele said no, and added grimly, "Don't worry, I won't fall asleep again." The Scotsman nodded and went out. He had taken no more than a few steps when a disagreeable thought struck him. Up until then he had been sure about the time element but after all how sure was that—absolutely sure? According to the broken watch in Gomez's pocket, stopped apparently when he had fallen to the ground out there in the courtyard, he had been struck down at nineteen minutes of six—which had given Steele a clean bill of health because of the distance of the hacienda from the public road where he had almost run Steele down. Suppose Gomez had been attacked a good deal earlier and the watch hands put forward, moved on deliberately . . . He wasn't enough of an expert himself to make certain.

The idea was a disturbing one. If there was anything in it, leaving Steele to guard Gomez was as good as dumping a brace of rabbits into a lettuce bed. He almost turned back —but there was that flight of someone from the lumber room above as he and Steele entered it, there was certainly no doubt about that . . . Moreover he was anxious to talk to the various people here at once. Make it quick.

The kitchen first, he didn't go into the living room where he could hear Speaker hammering. A door, the door through which they had carried Gomez earlier, was nearer.

Mrs. Tafoya and Mrs. Fergusson were both in the kitchen. Mrs. Tafoya was reading a book near the fire, head bent, shoulders humped, steel-rimmed glasses perched on her nose. Mrs. Fergusson on a straight chair close to the center table was leaning down putting on a pair of slippers.

Mrs. Fergusson had been out. A pair of muddy boots stood at the far end of the hearth, and a scarf and the heavy tweed coat she had taken off were hung on another chair near the stove. They were both wet. Mrs. Tafoya didn't look up when McKee opened the door but Mrs. Fergusson did. The same cool stare, the same poise; she showed no discomposure at McKee's questions. She said calmly that she had been in the courtyard filling a five-gallon can with kerosene for the lamps, the barrel was under a portal there. You weren't allowed to have the oil tank in the house in New Mexico, someone had told her. Anyhow it was very inconvenient—particularly in such weather. Mr. Jackson had gone with her and was filling another one. Her can was in the back entry. She waved a hand.

Before that? Was there a gleam of mockery in her?— an unspoken "You can't catch me this way. I'm not as green

as I look, I know how to protect myself." Various things,
she said indifferently, mopping up the mess that rancher
friend of the Danes had left in the living room, washing out
the mop in the scullery, getting fresh stockings and her slippers from her bedroom.

He turned to Mrs. Tafoya, whose clothes were dry.
She had been in her room reading "until it got too cold.
Then I came in here. My arthritis . . . The fire feels good."
She smiled at him timidly, adjusting her glasses. She had
been in the kitchen for the last five minutes or so.

So Mr. Jackson, the sleeping beauty, had roused. He
came in through the back door then, lugging a can of oil,
put it beside Mrs. Fergusson's in the entry, hung his dripping hat and coat there, took off galoshes stained with mud
and came toward the hearth smiling genially and rubbing
his hands. He was in his forties, a round comfortable man
of considerable girth with thinning dark hair parted neatly
on the side, practically no neck, and a good-natured plump
face.

"Who, me—for the last hour?"

He stared interrogatively at McKee but answered pleasantly. "Well, let's see now, let's see. After I got here and
had a lay-down, I had me a bath, or tried to, in the bathroom
upstairs. Say—you ought to take a look at it." He chuckled
and shook his head. "It's out of the ark, positively, and then
some. Oh, brother. The tub's half a mile long and the water's
a trickle. Rusted pipes I guess. Haven't been cleaned since
it was installed. Must have been a showpiece then. The old
Saturday night scrub-off sure makes sense in this dump.
Yes, sir, it sure does . . ."

Everything about Mr. Jackson was affable except his
eyes. They were small, pale, and knowing, with a twinkle
to them. He explained that he was on his way from Flagstaff
to Albuquerque to a sales meeting when he turned into El
Toro because of the storm, and because one of his tires was
going flat and he knew he'd never make it to Albuquerque

that night. "My card, sir." He took a square of pasteboard out of a wallet in his pocket and handed it to McKee with a bow. Mr. Harold Jackson was in ladies' foundations.

"This lady here," he waved at Mrs. Fergusson and gave another little bow, "was kind enough to say I might stay the night. Very good of her." The other people in the house? "The only ones I saw was her," he indicated Mrs. Tafoya, bent over her book again and apparently engrossed in it, "and a young lad, Ward I think his name is."

Mr. Jackson had never so much as heard of the Danes. He was new out here, a regular greenhorn. He had only recently been transferred from their branch in Brockton, Massachusetts, and had been in the Southwest less than a month.

"Nice country," he said largely. "Strange though. Indians, you know, and horses—and those mesas, elegant. They kind of get you. I think I'm going to like it out here when I get the hang of things. Of course it will take time. But I say when you're doing a thing do it right. Get to know your territory down to the grass-roots. It pays off in the end. Yes, sir." His little shrewd eyes, not unlike a pig's, continued to size up the Scotsman. "You from out around here yourself, mister—the sheriff maybe?"

It was mild, but it was a challenge of sorts. McKee said no. "Like you I come from the East." He was sure either Mrs. Tafoya or Mrs. Fergusson had heard Hilliard's greeting to him by his usual title earlier in the evening. "I'm an officer in the New York police department."

Jackson was delighted. "New York, huh? . . . Great town, great town, only wish I could have gotten into it more. In the police, eh?" He insisted on shaking hands. "Out here on business are you? Oh—just going to visit a friend. I thought you might be the sheriff because Mrs. Fergusson was telling me about a poor old guy who used to work here on this place that someone tried to knock off. You don't quite expect that in these parts. Peaceful. But

then I don't know, when you come to think about it . . .
Kit Carson—and Indians, cowboys with guns, and cattle
wars. Real tough underneath I guess. The old guy who was
hurt's a Mex, is he?"

A flicker of distaste could be seen crossing Mrs. Tafoya's half-averted face. McKee said, "A Spanish-American,
I believe. Yes."

"How's he doing, Captain?"

McKee lit a cigarette. A dead Emilio Gomez was on
the bill of fare for someone. It could very well be Mary
Dane apparently off in the blue—but better be on the safe
side. If the would-be killer thought Gomez was going to
die anyhow, there would be no need to help him over the
last mile. He shrugged. "If the poor fellow lasts another
couple of hours, I'll be surprised. But by morning the state
police ought to be here, and they'll take over."

He hadn't meant it as reassurance, nor did it have that
effect. There was a general tightening, barely perceptible,
but there, in all three of them. Jackson said slowly, "The
state police, eh? But the phone's out." The Scotsman explained that Speaker, a neighboring rancher, was going to
try and get word to them. He lived nearer the barracks.
Fire and lamplight on the whitewashed walls, smoky in
places. The noise of the storm. Above it in a lull a horse
whinnied somewhere. The sound came through a window
over the sink that was raised two or three inches from the
bottom. Mrs. Fergusson got up, shut the window and went
over to the stove on which a big pot of coffee was perking.

"A cup, Inspector?"

So she did know who he was . . . McKee declined.
"Not now, thanks—perhaps later."

"I'm your man," Jackson said heartily. "Great stuff,
coffee. I'm a regular coffee hound myself. Can't get enough
of it. I always say there's nothing like it for a real pick-me-
up." Mrs. Tafoya remained as buried in her reading as
though she were alone on a desert island. A woman without

curiosity—apparently engrossed in her book. McKee left them in search of the others, Henry Hilliard and the two women.

In the shadowy dining room he paused. Off on the right the living room was in darkness. Speaker must have finished with the door and gone. Straight ahead was a small room to which the lamp had been removed. Hilliard was there, and Jill Sheppard and Mrs. Mole in chairs close to the hearth. Above the salt and below the salt, young Ward was the liaison man between the two groups. The little room, a sort of study, had a corner fireplace. He was down on one knee mending the fire with some fresh logs, and he and Hilliard were chatting.

Ward said, "You knew the Danes, didn't you, Mr. Hilliard? Do you remember a Mollie Santo who used to work for them a long time ago?"

"Santo . . . Santo." Hilliard frowned reflectively. "I don't think—yes, I believe I do, just dimly."

"She's my mother, sir. Santo was her maiden name."
"Oh?"

"Yes. After she left the Danes she married my father and they settled up in Rosita. I never saw my father, he died before I was born and later on Ma married again. Anyhow she used to talk about the Danes a lot . . . The one they call Miss Mary came to see us a couple of times in Rosita when I was just a kid. But I remember the big box of candy she brought. It had a pink ribbon tied around in a big bow. Funny thing. Ma was to have come down here on a visit not long ago and I was to have come with her, but she got sick and had to go to the hospital. When I saw the name Dane on the mailbox outside the gates I thought of Miss Mary and turned in. But she wasn't here."

Behind the drawn curtains rain dashed furiously at the windows. Ward said, putting the poker into the stand, "Gee, I wish it would let up . . . I'm anxious to get south as fast as I can and get a job. I hope it's over by morning."

Hilliard hoped so, too. "These mountain storms don't generally last very long, the earth's so dry and the runoff's fast." Reclining gracefully in her chair, the most comfortable chair in the room, Mrs. Mole shivered. She was bored and fretful. "I simply can't *stand* this horrid place indefinitely, Henry. I simply *can't*."

"Now, Rita," her young sister told her, replacing a book she had taken from one of the low cases lining the walls. "Stop making a fuss. What good does it do—and it's not Henry's fault, is it? Who was it who insisted on leaving Denver this morning? . . . I like storms. They're exciting."

She looked very pretty with her flushed cheeks and fair hair. Young Ward, picking up the empty woodbasket, gave her a glance of shy admiration. He was starting out of the little room as the Scotsman entered it. McKee stopped him. If he could only find three or even two people who had been together during the half hour he and Speaker had been in the stables, it would be a help.

No soap. For the next five minutes he kept saying, "Yes, I see . . . Yes." As with the three in the kitchen, "Pray hold me excused." None of them had been together for any length of time during the interval in question. Hilliard had remained in the drawing room for a few minutes and had then moved in here. With a high wind like this the big room was impossible to heat. Mrs. Mole had gone up to her bedroom to change into a warmer dress. Although one didn't expect, in ordinary houses at this time of year . . . The haughty, slightly overweight beauty looked at McKee coldly, smoothing folds of brown wool. Yes, her sister had been with her part of the time. No, they didn't have the same room, their rooms adjoined.

Jill Sheppard had been around and about the hacienda doing a little exploring, she said the place absolutely fascinated her. She had never seen anything remotely like it before. She'd like to live in it for a while, get the feel of it—

maybe one would see ghosts, at which remark Rita Mole gave a low anguished moan of protest. Young Ward had been making himself generally useful, getting wood, filling lamps and so forth.

"What makes you ask, Inspector?" Hilliard's glance at McKee was keen.

"Because someone entered the room we put Gomez in while Mr. Speaker and I were out in the stables."

Hilliard was concerned. "Emilio was alone? If I'd known I would gladly have—"

McKee said Mr. Steele had been with Gomez but unfortunately Steele had fallen asleep. It was while he was asleep that whoever had entered the room had extinguished the lamp.

At the mention of Steele's name the girl's eyes opened wide. "Steele?" she said, in an oddly stiff tone, and the Scotsman nodded.

"Yes. We met on the main road outside the ranch gates and arrived here together. He's a writer from New York here on a trip."

"I see." It was all she said, her gaze averted.

"But Emilio's all right?" Hilliard wanted to know.

McKee said dryly, "As right as he'll ever be unless we can get a doctor for him very soon. Otherwise I'm afraid—" He was grim.

It was all too much for Mrs. Mole. This time her outburst was almost hysterical. "I *told* you so, Henry, I told you so. I knew something terrible was going to happen. This house is horrible, it's evil . . . You can feel it. I felt it instinctively from the first moment we came in. I'm sensitive . . . It would have been better to spend the night in the car. Anything would have been better—anything. And it will be hours and hours until morning. I don't think I can *stand* it . . ."

Soothing words from Hilliard, curter ones from the girl; McKee left her to them and went to check on Gomez.

The long drawing room was cold but the pane in the front door had been mended and wind and rain no longer drove in. He didn't immediately enter the room that had been Veronica Dane's. He tapped on the door and Steele answered alertly through it. Gomez was just the same.

McKee said, "With you in a minute," and advanced along the corridor to take a look at the photographs Speaker had said were hung there. It would be interesting to see what the late Veronica Dane had looked like—and Mary Dane. Very much Mary Dane. There was only one certainty in this whole business. Someone had tried to wipe out Emilio Gomez, and had all but succeeded—*and* Mary had taken her departure from the ranch in a great hurry, leaving her gauntlets behind her in her anxiety to get clear of El Toro. She could be far away by now in spite of the storm. She was used to weather out here and mounted on a horse she could go places a car couldn't even attempt.

The first picture he came to was an enlarged photograph of Veronica Dane, a handsome gray-haired woman with a splendid carriage, mounted on an Arabian horse. Arrogant, sure of herself, a lady who would always be right. "Veronica knows best . . . It's for your own good . . . This hurts me more than it does you." He studied her face. There was pride and ruthlessness in the poise of the rather large head, the modeling of mouth and jaw and chin. Three more pictures of her confirmed this impression. In the fifth she was with an older man and woman, probably her parents. There were a couple of dogs with her. One of them was evidently the Dalmatian, Spot, who had disappeared the day she died.

Moving his light on, McKee held it steady on nothing, or rather, on a blank space on the wall from which a picture had been removed, recently. The plaster was a different color. Another photograph had hung there. There were more of them farther along. There was no photograph of Mary, with or without other members of her family.

Whistling softly McKee looked around. There was an outside door a few yards away at the end of the corridor. It was locked, but if Mary had kept back a set of keys she could have slipped in here after laying Gomez low and before she took off . . .

He started thoughtfully back along the corridor. He had all but reached the room in which Gomez lay when the door was yanked open. Steele stood in the opening. He said in a low voice, "It's Speaker," and waved toward one of the windows. Speaker was standing outside the window, lantern in hand. While Steele relocked the door McKee crossed the floor, pushed back the stiff catch and opened the window. Speaker clambered over the sill bringing wind and rain in with him. His clothes were saturated, his boots thick with mud. He had been running, his breathing was short.

Emptying the water out of his hat brim unceremoniously on the tiled floor he said, "I left the pick-up down the road—thought I'd better shut up about it till I saw you. I found Polo. The saddle's empty. Got her tied to the car. No sign of Mary anywhere."

Polo—it took only a second for the name to register. Polo was the horse Mary had ridden over to El Toro, and presumably ridden away on in flight. Mary hadn't ridden away. She was still somewhere close at hand.

4

Mary Dane was definitely not in the hacienda. McKee enlisted Hilliard's aid. They had gone through the house cursorily before, they went over it again with a fine tooth comb while Steele remained with Emilio Gomez. After he had delivered his startling news Speaker left almost at once, taking the piebald, Polo, with him. He went reluctantly, because he had to. It was of the first importance that the police be notified as soon as possible of the state of affairs at El Toro and he said that the Chavez, the creek he had to cross, was probably already up. If it overflowed its banks he wouldn't be able to get across at all. It practically looped the place. Moreover, the arroyos along his route would probably be in full spate, washing out long sections of the road. Only last year a woman and two boys in a car had been swept to their deaths not far from the El Toro gates in a flash flood. The car and their bodies hadn't been found for a week in a lower valley a mile to the west.

"Well, Mary certainly isn't anywhere in this house," Hilliard said tiredly at the end of a half-hour's intensive search. Every room had been entered, every wardrobe—

there were very few closets—gone through without result. Only the outbuildings remained.

They consisted of the barn and attached stables, a wash house, the cold room where meat was stored in winter, a chicken house and various other structures, some of them no longer in use. Two men armed with lanterns, and with the possibility of someone retreating before their advance, couldn't hope to do a really adequate job until daylight came. But meanwhile some sort of preliminary check had to be attempted.

Mrs. Fergusson and her other uninvited lodgers for the night knew what had happened. They had to know under the circumstances. Mr. Jackson and young Ward had offered to help, but McKee declined. Someone had to stay with the women, he said. Mrs. Mole was in a state of near collapse at this latest development of a riderless horse and a missing woman. Mrs. Fergusson was black-browed and stony-faced. Even the girl, Jill Sheppard, looked nervous and ill at ease.

After arraying themselves in boots and slickers in the scullery beyond the kitchen McKee and Hilliard started out. Leaving the room Hilliard said, "What I don't get, Inspector, is why Mary came back here to El Toro in a storm like this. She said in the note she left for the Speakers it was to get something important she had forgotten. But surely you'd think she'd have waited until morning to start out. She knew Mrs. Fergusson wasn't going to run away. And she isn't an impetuous woman, at least not as I recall. Also, when she did get here, why didn't she come into the house? I'm worried about her, seriously worried."

McKee was, too. His only answer was a shrug, and they plodded on through the courtyard, shoulders hunched against the drive of the wind and the slashing rain. They tried the chicken house first, then the wash house. Nothing. No one. They couldn't get into the cold room. It didn't matter. Mary Dane was obviously not in there. It was padlocked on the outside and there were no windows. Wet leaves that had clung to the branches through the winter were coming down from the cottonwoods and littering the mud; the going was slippery. They took the barn and stables last—and there a mystery confronted them.

The old black mare, on which young Ward had ridden bareback for help and which he had left standing docilely in the rear courtyard, head down droopingly, was in one of the stalls in the stable, munching contentedly on hay. McKee stared at the black horse fixedly. "How the *hell*—" he said softly and explained to Hilliard that the doors of the place were all closed when he and Speaker left the stables earlier that night. "How the devil did that horse manage to get in here?"

Hilliard suggested that one of the numerous doors might have blown open and then shut and McKee nodded doubtfully. That could be it. But there was another possibility. The lurking man or woman Mrs. Mole thought she had seen outside the living-room window three or four hours ago might have come in here for some purpose or other and the mare might have followed whoever it was in. Drawn by the lamplight something or someone had certainly been outside that window trying to see in, as witness the broken twigs underneath it. It could have been Mary Dane . . . The two men went on with their search.

Back in the hacienda in the room where Gomez lay with no change in his harsh breathing, Steele paced the floor restlessly. Now that he was alone he didn't have to school his face or voice or expression. He was savagely angry. The anger had been building up in him all evening. It was directed at himself. He was a fool to have come west at all, a goddamned triple-plated idiot. The situation in which he had landed when he had walked into this place was nobody's fault but his own. He should have been able to take what lay behind it in stride, toss it over his shoulder

. . . Water under the bridge. Let it go—and to hell with it. But unfortunately he was here and the only thing to do now was to keep himself to himself and get away as soon as possible . . . Actually being isolated and shut up alone in the room with the wounded yardman was a godsend.

But he didn't remain alone. He was on his fifth cigarette in as many minutes when there was a knock on the door. Steele stiffened, then made his muscles relax. It was probably the Inspector coming back. But better be sure. He went over to the door and spoke through it. "Yes? Who is it?"

A woman answered. It was Mrs. Tafoya. He opened the door a crack. Mrs. Tafoya was carrying a wicker basket filled with blanket-wrapped bottles full of hot water and young Ward was behind her with a load of logs for the fire.

Mrs. Tafoya said in her bumbling voice, "I thought— the other bottles, the ones he has, would be getting cold and he'd need more heat . . ." Steele hesitated. But there was safety in numbers. She and young Ward could scarcely be in collusion, they were or seemed to be strangers to each other, and what the woman said was true.

He pulled the door wider and let them in. Ward went over and dumped the logs in the woodbox and Mrs. Tafoya began carefully taking out the old bottles from under the blankets and replacing them with the new ones. The room was big and shadowy outside the circle of lamplight and it was difficult to keep an eye on both of them at once. Nevertheless it was a relief to think of other things besides his own position.

With the news about Mary Dane, that she had managed to reach the hacienda and in all probability was still close by, the picture had altered menacingly and the slightest detail might be of importance. Somebody might be helping her for instance, could be in collusion with her. Did the Tafoya woman give a glance at the desk and the tapestry behind it that concealed the door and the staircase leading to the lumber room above? He couldn't be sure. He wondered again where they had come into contact earlier because he was surer than ever that they had . . .

Her task completed, and the covers smoothed and neatly back in place, she stood beside the bed looking down at the stricken Gomez, deep in coma. She was sideways to Steele. In profile her features looked different. They were clean and well cut. He revised his opinion about her age. Her stance, and general carriage, made her look well on in her fifties, she could be at least a decade younger . . .

As though she felt the weight of his scrutiny she turned her head and the look of youth, comparative youth, was instantly erased. "Poor man, poor man," she said, shaking her head pityingly. "Does—does the Inspector think there's any hope for him, sir?"

Listening to her, Steele felt an odd little thrill shoot along his nerves. It wasn't the words. It was the timbre of her voice. Some cadence in it struck a cord in him. Yes, he had not only seen this woman somewhere before, he had heard her talk . . . But where? And when, and under what circumstances? Try as he would it refused to come. He didn't get a glimmer. Aloud, he said, "I'm afraid he hasn't too much of a chance unless we get hold of a doctor pretty soon."

Ward had turned and was also staring at Gomez from the foot of the bed. He was too young to have seen much of impending death and it palpably awed him. The freckles stood out prominently on his lean face. "If only there was something we could *do* for the poor old guy," he said.

Steele merely shrugged. Everything that could be done here on the spot was being done. Mrs. Tafoya adjusted her glasses and picked up her basket holding the bottles she had removed and a moment later they were both gone. Steele settled down somberly to his vigil again after relocking the door behind them. Where the devil was McKee? He had been gone a hell of a long time. What was keeping him so long?

The thing keeping the Scotsman was the unexpected discovery he and Hilliard made in the barn. It came at the last moment.

About to leave the stables proper the Scotsman lingered. The mystery of how the black horse had managed to get into the place continued to bother him. The doors, three in number—one led to the barn, one into the rambling courtyard and the third into the fenced-in corral at the back. Both these last were closed. Like Speaker earlier, Hilliard had tried to soothe Veronica's stallion, and with no better success. The big brute rolled a red eye and kept on bucking and kicking out viciously. Suddenly a remark of Speaker's when they were here before came back to McKee. Speaker had said, "I don't know why Carlo's not in his own loose box."

The loose box was two stalls down. McKee returned to it. It was big and roomy, and the one nearest the corral door. A bucket half filled with water in a corner, the feed box with hay in it, and a bed of piled straw covering part of the floor. The straw was fresh, a clear gold in the light of the lantern Hilliard carried. There was no apparent reason why Carlo had taken a dislike to his usual quarters, none whatever. Quite the contrary . . .

McKee stepped into the loose box, switched on his flashlight and sent more light this way and that. Puzzled, Hilliard watched him frowningly from the entrance to the stall. McKee had paused beside the straw bed. It was a good six feet in length by four or five wide. He scrutinized it narrow-eyed, then he was down on one knee and had begun pulling the straw away, tossing it aside in armfuls. His hands burrowed deeper. "There's something here," he said over his shoulder into the gloom, and Hilliard joined him.

There was indeed something there. The first thing the Scotsman uncovered was a foot, a woman's foot in a short

riding boot. A hoarse exclamation from Hilliard. The foot
was Mary Dane's. Mary Dane was lying there, under cling-
ing wisps of straw, partly on her face, her head half turned,
and Mary Dane was dead. She was not only dead, she had
been dead for some hours. Rigor had already begun to set in.

5

The drum of rain outside, on the roof
and against the walls was loud. The eldritch screech of the
wind; it retreated wailingly, preparing for a fresh onslaught.
In the inner stillness the stallion nickered and pawed rough
boarding. Hilliard said, "God . . ." and put a hand on the
side of the stall for support. McKee made a brief examination of the body. Whatever doubt, if there was any as to
the cause of Veronica Dane's death, there was none where
her younger sister was concerned. Mary had been killed
deliberately. It was homicide—no question about that. A
thin piece of leather, part of a lariat, had been flung over
her head from behind and the noose pulled tight. Asphyxia-
tion. She had been strangled to death. Her face was swollen,
puffy, and the skin was suffused. It hadn't taken long to
kill her. It would have been a matter of a very few mo-
ments . . .

Henry Hilliard's usual composure had broken wide
open. He was badly shaken. His skin was pallid and he
looked as though he were going to be sick.

"God!" he said again. "The brutality of it. It's horrible.

I can't—it's hard to *believe* . . . Mary . . . Who would want . . . And why? . . . It's simply incredible to me."

It might be incredible, McKee thought, but it was true. In spite of the chill—they could see their breaths—Hilliard's forehead was wet. He wiped it with an unsteady hand. "As far as I know she never did any harm to anyone in her whole life. Never. She wasn't that sort. If it had been Veronica now—"

Fernandez's comment in another shape; McKee rose to his feet. "Perhaps not, but Mary Dane got in someone's way, anyhow. That much is clear." He spoke in an absent tone, his mind busy. A pattern was forming . . . Unlike Emilio Gomez, Mary wore no watch but from the presence of rigor he was convinced that she had died before Gomez was attacked and got that possibly lethal blow in the courtyard outside the hacienda. Had the yardman been a witness of Mary's murder?

He frowned. From what he had heard of the yardman, Gomez would scarcely have stood idly by while one of his former mistresses was being killed before taking to his heels with the perpetrator in pursuit of him. Gomez had fled in the direction of the house, probably to give the alarm, to get help. Before he could do so he had been overtaken, and stopped summarily with that blow . . . Very well. Grant this. Then what? If Gomez hadn't been actually on the scene when the loop of lariat was thrown over Mary Dane's head and pulled taut, where had he been?

The Scotsman picked up the lantern and sent yellow light around. There was a small window in each stall giving on the corral . . . He nodded. That could be it. Gomez might have been outside one of these windows looking in and had seen what was happening. By the time he had managed to get round here and into the stables Mary's body might have been in process of being disposed of under the concealing straw.

McKee raised the lantern higher and his glance sharpened. The window in the loose box where the dead woman lay had a small triangle of glass out of one of the lower panes . . . The yardman might have heard as well as seen . . . That "Miss Mary" of his at the end of the short labored sentence, which he himself had half taken as an accusation of Mary was not that at all . . . No. Gomez had wanted to tell them about her, about the fate that had overtaken her and where she was. Then what of the words that went before, "Not—" and a mumbled name, Perez, Patrick, Peter . . . ?

McKee gave it up for the moment. The first thing to do was have another look around this whole place in the light of what they had found—or rather the darkness—enigma piled on enigma. He turned away.

Hilliard was leaning against the boards at the end of the stall. He stood erect with an effort. He said, "But aren't you going to—hadn't we better move her? We can't just—we could carry her into the tackroom, couldn't we?"

McKee shook his head. "No. It wouldn't do Miss Dane any good, she's beyond caring, far beyond. And besides she can't be touched. She's got to be left there just as she is now, just as we found her, until the coroner or medical examiner, whatever they have out here, has a look at the body and gives his verdict for the record."

It bothered Hilliard, didn't suit his sense of fitness. "But—you're a police official, Inspector? Surely—"

McKee said, "No, Mr. Hilliard," and explained. "I have no official status in this state, absolutely none. I have to obey the law like everyone else. As far as New Mexico goes I have no more authority than that of any other private citizen—and that doesn't include moving the body of a murdered woman."

Hilliard looked at him and drew a long breath. He was beginning to get his control back and he was a sensible man. He said reluctantly, "I suppose you're right," and followed McKee out of the loose box. The Scotsman began a reëxamination of the entire rambling structure, the stable itself first, then the barn beyond. In the big central enclosure bales of hay were piled in great blocks bound with wire, and bags of oats and a couple of bran were stacked against one wall. There was a huge mound of oats covered by a cap of wire mesh against another, and various farm implements were clustered in corners, pitchforks and shovels and crowbars, a rusty harrow and a small threshing machine. None of these was informative.

The stables behind, the tackroom on one side, the little room in which Emilio Gomez had slept on the other; McKee went into this room. Gomez's accommodations had certainly not been luxurious to say the least. A camp bed covered with blankets, work clothes on pegs behind a curtain, a single battered chair with a rung missing from the back, and a wooden shelf on which stood a tin basin, a bar of yellow soap in the top of a can cover, and a brown towel on a nail. There was no heat and the chill was bone-piercing.

Gomez had been a neat man. Everything was in immaculate order except for the cot. The blankets on it were tossed about in disarray. McKee went over to it. According to Mrs. Fergusson the yardman had left El Toro very early the morning before to tote stuff up to his sister's in Chimayo, or so Mary Dane had told her before she took her departure.

McKee slid a hand between the blankets, felt around and held his hand still. Warmth under his palm, not very much of it but nevertheless warmth. Someone had been lying on the cot with the covers drawn up, recently. He threw the top two blankets back. Warmth—and wetness. There were smears of mud on the coarse sheet near the bottom of the cot where two boot heels had rested not long ago. The mud was still damp.

McKee glanced at Hilliard. "Mrs. Mole's apparition I think. The man she saw looking in through the window earlier tonight. Seems like it anyhow, at a glance.

Hilliard was still occupied with the dreadful spectacle

of Mary Dane back in the stables. At the Scotsman's remark he roused himself, came to attention. "Mrs. Mole's—Oh, I see what you mean. Yes. What she saw was a tramp seeking shelter from the storm in here later, perhaps?"

McKee definitely thought so. He had already envisioned someone slipping away before their advancing light when they first dashed out of the house that night, someone watching them from darkness ready to dart this way or that. He said, "Yes," and after going over the tackroom again without discovering anything new the two men left the barn and started across the driveway to the hacienda. Rain, wind, the threshing of unseen branches; plowing along head down, the Scotsman was scarcely aware of the storm.

One murder, signed, sealed and delivered, one attempted murder; the people showing, the people who because they were on the scene could have a hand in it—and no one could be excluded at the moment—were Hilliard, Mrs. Mole, her sister Jill Sheppard, Mrs. Fergusson, Mrs. Tafoya, young Ward, the jovial Mr. Jackson and now the unknown occupier of Gomez's bed. Steele was an outside possibility. Whether or not, what they badly hadn't needed was another individual added to those already on hand. Definitely not.

When Hilliard and McKee got into the house, late as it was, and tired as the other occupants all were, no one had gone to bed. It was as if, without knowing, they clung together either for protection or out of mutual distrust. The two men got rid of their boots and slickers in the scullery. While they did so they talked. Hilliard was almost himself again. Forceful, decisive, a man used to dealing with emergencies. He wanted to know whether the Scotsman was going to break the news of Mary Dane's death to the others.

McKee thought for a moment. If the killer was under the roof he would know all about Mary. But the rest of them wouldn't—and panic, at that hour, was definitely something to be avoided in an isolated house cut off from communication with the outside world . . . He said not immediately, anyhow, and Hilliard looked relieved.

"Rita's—Mrs. Mole's—bad enough as it is now, but if she should hear about this, about poor Mary"—he threw up his hands—"she'll really cut loose."

McKee was anxious to get back to Gomez to see whether there had been any change in his condition, any improvement, however slight. If only the yardman recovered, enough at least to be able to talk, they might get somewhere. He left the scullery and hurried along the corridor.

Steele opened quickly at his knock, relocked the door after him. The moment the Scotsman crossed to the bed and looked at Gomez his heart sank.

6

"He seems worse to me, too," Steele said heavily.

"Yes, we'll try another shot of adrenalin."

The drug had no immediate effect. While they watched the gray, deeply wrinkled old face, the Scotsman said, "Anything happen here?" Steele said nothing much, and told him about the appearance of Mrs. Tafoya with fresh bottles of hot water and Ward with firewood. A little later Mrs. Fergusson had come herself with an offer of coffee and something to eat. She had said she'd sit with Gomez herself while he got it. Steele said dryly, "I wasn't having any. You didn't find Miss Dane?"

"Oh yes, we found her." Beside the bed, fingers on Gomez's pulse, McKee described the discovery he and Hilliard had made in the loose box in the stables.

"Good Lord—Mary Dane dead—strangled to death . . ." The writer stared at him. He was bemused. "Seems as though there's a spell over this place . . . Then it wasn't Mary who removed that picture presumably of herself from the wall out there in the hall?"

McKee shrugged. "It certainly doesn't look like it, although she might have done so earlier, when she first got here, provided she had another set of keys besides the two she surrendered to Mrs. Fergusson. But there were no keys on her." He went on with the rest of it.

In his opinion Gomez had been struck down after Mary Dane died—because of the rigor. Of course outside temperatures had an effect on the advance of it, and the stables were cold, but the straw with which her body was closely covered would have retained a certain amount of heat. In addition, there was the individual who had taken refuge in Emilio Gomez's blankets in the yardman's room in the barn, and who must have been there when he and Hilliard first entered the building. He raised a shoulder. Of course, whoever it was might have had nothing to do with any killing, might have been keeping under cover for some other reason entirely. It was hard to say at that point—anyhow, first find your hare, which would be exceedingly difficult under the circumstances. The slam of rain against the dark window-panes emphasized his words.

"God, what a kettle of fish, Inspector," Steele exclaimed, galvanized out of his ordinary impassivity.

The Scotsman agreed absently. Any hope of immediate enlightenment lay with the badly wounded Gomez, and listening to the breathing coming through his open mouth, Gomez was on his last legs or dangerously close to it. Unless help arrived soon there was precious little chance of his ever speaking again. He put the lax weather-beaten hand back under the covers gently and smoked a cigarette, walking restlessly around the room.

Steele watched him out of eyes red-rimmed with fatigue. "If there was only something—what are you going to do, Inspector? Talk to these people again?"

McKee flicked ash into the fire Ward had built up. "A waste of time as things are. They're stuck with the stories they've already told, and they'll stay with them. They know nothing, heard nothing, saw nothing. Anything else would be stupid and not one of them is that, not by a long shot. Sit on it is about all we *can* do, until morning anyhow. By then Speaker may be able to contact the state police . . ." He studied Steele's thin ugly clever face and said quietly, "You're not holding anything back by any chance, are you?"

Steele didn't rise to the bait. He showed neither indignation nor confusion, nor did he protest too much. "What are you getting at, Inspector? You and I were together out on the public road the better part of a mile from here when Gomez was struck down, to say nothing of what took place previously and that poor Miss Dane and what happened to her. You know that yourself. And as far as this place goes— and that unfortunate old fellow, and the Dane family—I never heard of any of them in my life until we were unlucky enough to turn through those gates and walk up that driveway."

He sounded as though he was speaking the truth. "But you did think you'd seen Mrs. Tafoya before."

"Oh, that, yes, I did—and do, but for the life of me I can't remember where."

"Don't worry it and it may come of its own accord. Memory's a tricky thing. Now better go and get yourself something to eat and a cup of coffee, and bring me coffee when you come back, will you? Black—no sugar. I'll hold the fort here."

"Right." Steele went out. It was a relief to get away from the figure in the bed if only for a short time, and yet— The hell with it. He didn't care who he ran into. He made his way slowly down the corridor, across the drawing room and through the archway into the dining room. There was some visibility there from an oil lamp turned low on the long carved table.

Without knowing precisely why, he came to a stop

near the table. What had brought him to a halt? Something certainly. Some sound he had picked up, which registered through his preoccupation? It must have been that.

He looked around but there was no one in sight and nothing to be heard except the storm beyond the walls. And yet, his scalp prickled a little, he had a feeling that there was someone near him. He stooped and looked under the table and then into the little room beyond where there was a handful of glow behind a fire screen. Nobody. There was only one other place, the locked closet in the wall on the far side of the windows. He went over and tried the door. It was still locked. Imagination, he told himself impatiently and walked on across the pantry and into the kitchen.

Mrs. Tafoya was the only one there. She looked up at him through the steel-rimmed glasses, nodded indifferently and returned to her book. The ticking of a clock, a cheap alarm clock, on a shelf, the steady downpour beyond the windows, an occasional crack from a log on the fire. Steele fixed himself a sandwich, there was a ham on a counter, and butter and a pile of bread. He ate voraciously, on his feet. The last food he had had was at a wayside dump at noon and not much then. Finished, he rinsed his plate at the sink, and poured himself coffee. He made a certain amount of noise but Mrs. Tafoya didn't once look up or speak. Apparently she had no interest whatever in her surroundings or in him. The silence was heavy, oppressive.

Finally he addressed her round-shouldered back. "The others gone to bed?" he asked pleasantly.

She didn't turn. "I don't know. I guess so." A woman of few words; her drab voice was flat, toneless.

Steele gazed at her bent head speculatively. Could he be wrong? Could he have imagined that note in it earlier that night, an odd remembered note with a peculiar timbre to it? No, but she had been swayed by emotion then, looking at Gomez . . . The swinging door from the pantry started to open. Did the clumsy figure by the hearth draw itself together? Steele swung around.

It was Mrs. Mole who came in.

She stopped dead when she saw him. A ringed hand went to the throat of the padded green satin robe she wore over soft white slippers. There was blank astonishment in her wide stare, and fear, and the leap of hatred. Her reddened lips seemed to have gone dry. She passed the tip of her tongue over them and swallowed. She looked at Mrs. Tafoya, and then back at Steele.

"Oh—" she said, "I didn't expect—didn't know that—that there was anyone here . . ."

She was a dithering calf. No, she was too old for that, a cow. She was also a knave in Steele's book, greedy, sly, unscrupulous, and an unmitigated liar. She started to turn away from his bland gaze.

"Don't go," he said genially. "Don't you know me, Mrs. Mole? Surely you must . . . I used to work with your husband in New York, and we met there half a dozen times. Don't you remember me?"

Was she going to try and brazen it out, he wondered? She couldn't do that with certain parts of it. She was pulling herself together, trying to reach a decision. At last she spoke stiffly.

"Why—why it's Mr. Steele, isn't it? Of course. I didn't expect to—to see you out here, so far away . . ."

This was for the benefit of Mrs. Tafoya. His smile was openly derisive. It infuriated her. Rage made her make up her mind. Her hands were thrust into the pockets of her robe and her head was high. She went on icily. "I think, Mr. Steele, considering all the circumstances, the less we see of each other, the better. I should think your own sense of —of decency would tell you that."

Steele remained cool. After all it was more or less what was to be expected from her. She was going to play it the haughty way. Injured innocence. "Unhand me, villain."

Realistically there was no other stand she could take.

He had an ace in the hole it was true, an ace however in a game already lost . . . He said, "Circumstances sometimes change, Mrs. Mole—but as you wish," and made her a little bow. A hard right to the jaw, it drove her from the field. She left the kitchen fast, sweeping out regally.

Steele went slowly over to the stove, and poured two mugs of coffee, another for himself and one for McKee. The anger in him was deep. He was also bitterly amused. No change; if she had a conscience it had long since withered away. No, Rita Mole was following the old script, line for line, and she didn't mean to make any alterations or revisions. His intention had been to make her do so. But the original purpose of his journey out here to the Southwest— a cockeyed purpose anyhow, had been blunted by what had happened since his meeting with the Inspector. The tragedy and horror in this unholy place had given it proportion.

He put the coffeepot back on the stove tiredly. His own grievances, personal unhappiness, didn't seem nearly as important as they had back in New York. He had come out here to find Rita Mole and confront her, before witnesses, and wring the truth out of her at the point of a gun if necessary. Now although he was actually under the same roof with her and had the chance, what she had done, and she alone, no longer seemed to matter particularly.

He located the sugar bowl, and stirred sugar into his own mug. What had patience on a monument, reading at the hearth as though she were alone, thought of all this? He glanced toward her—and got a slight shock. She wasn't reading. She was watching him covertly. The black pane of a small window opening into the scullery gave back a perfect reflection of a good part of the room. She had been an observer of the brief confrontation between him and Rita Mole. Their eyes met for a flash and then she looked down at her book.

He had a notion to brace her but what could he say? "I believe we've met somewhere before?" It wasn't so. He had seen her and heard her but they hadn't met personally. Of that much he was sure. He said, "Good night, Mrs. Tafoya," and picked up the two mugs. "Good night, sir." She spoke over her shoulder, didn't turn. He left the kitchen and rejoined the Inspector in the room down the corridor.

Vigil at the bedside of the dying man. By fire and lamplight, with rain pouring down steadily and wind blowing hard outside the stout walls. It didn't sound as though it would ever stop. Gomez was sinking deeper and deeper into coma. McKee and Steele talked in snatches. No help could be expected before morning and by then in all probability it would be too late. By midnight the wind did begin to die down a little, its onslaught was less ferocious and the gusts were farther apart.

A couple of times Steele had a half-notion of telling McKee about Mrs. Mole and his own reason for being out here in New Mexico and on her trail. But to what purpose? What good would it do? It had nothing whatever to do with what had happened on this godforsaken ranch. And in any case when day came he would be off, headed east, destination Manhattan Island, County, City, and State of New York.

At around one Hilliard came. He tapped at the door and McKee opened it a foot or so. Hilliard said the ladies had gone to bed and asked if there was anything he could do, any way he could be of service. McKee thanked him and said no, not at the moment. Shortly after that Ward arrived with a fresh supply of wood. The young fellow looked tired. He had had a tough day walking up here from Albuquerque into the Sandias through the gathering storm. He avoided glancing toward the bed from which the harsh rattle of Gomez's breathing came.

Ward said the others, Mrs. Fergusson and Mrs. Tafoya and Mr. Jackson, like Mrs. Mole and Miss Sheppard, had all gone to their rooms, Mrs. Tafoya last. It was kind of lonely . . . From his tone he evidently didn't care for the hacienda any more than Steele did. He thought he'd go to bed himself, if the Inspector thought the wood he dumped in the wood basket would last the rest of the night. The Inspector did think so and Ward went, openly relieved at getting out of the room.

There were no further incursions after that. Presently Steele dozed off with Gomez's hard rattle in his ears. When he woke later it was to utter silence, outside and in. The rain had miraculously stopped and the wind was no longer blowing. There was nothing but the soft drip of water from the eaves. Steele could scarcely believe in the stillness. It was too good to be true. He sat up guiltily blinking sleep out of his eyes. The Inspector was on the other side of the room at the bed. He was drawing a sheet up over the yard-man's head.

"Dead?" Steele said, and the Scotsman nodded and looked at his watch. It was a few minutes after four.

Steele felt cold. Although they had expected Gomez to die it was still a shock. "Did he say anything, Inspector, be-fore—"

"Not a word." McKee completed his task. "Now, Steele," he went on, "if you feel equal to it we have a little work to do—but first I'll go and get young Ward."

7

"You mean—you mean you want me to stay here alone with him, sir?"

Ward glanced sideways toward the covered mound on the bed like a nervous horse. When the Scotsman roused him he had been deeply asleep in the little room off the kitchen and beyond the pantry that had formerly been the cook's. His shrinking from the task McKee wanted him to do was patent. Then he squared bony shoulders under the windbreaker he had pulled on. "O.K., Inspector."

McKee said, "Someone's got to stay here and see that nobody enters the room and touches anything. And we won't be long. Ready, Steele?"

Just as they were leaving the room McKee paused and asked Ward about the black horse he had been riding down the driveway when they first encountered him. "Did you put him in the stable when you came back from getting my bag out of my car?"

Ward said no, he hadn't. He had left him in the rear courtyard near the kitchen door. "I figured you were in a hurry like."

McKee nodded. The black horse was disposed of, he must have followed the man who had occupied Gomez's bed into the barn. Veronica's stallion remained as a question mark. Obviously the stallion hadn't been inside the stable in his own loose box when Mary Dane's body was placed under the bed of straw. Yet the stallion was there, in another stall, when he and the rancher made their preliminary abortive search—and that meant that the stranger had been somewhere outside on the ranch for some hours and that he must have made several forays during one of which the stallion, like the black horse, had managed to get into the barn and under cover in his wake.

McKee explained this to Steele after they left the room that had been Veronica Dane's and walked softly down the corridor.

"Sounds all right but—is it important?" Steele asked doubtfully, and McKee said yes, emphatically, that because of the time element it definitely added one more to the list of possible perpetrators.

The hacienda was now dark and silent except for a lamp in the kitchen and a handful of fire on the hearth there. Clad again in boots and slickers the two men made their way out through the back door which McKee locked behind him. What he wanted was a look at the cars the variegated crowd of people had arrived in. Four eyes were better than two, and whoever had retreated from the barn when he and Hilliard were in the process of discovering Mary's body, might have taken shelter in one of the cars for what remained of the night. Dawn wasn't far off, although up there in the mountains blocking the east it would be later than in the surrounding deserts.

There were three cars under the portal at the far side of the rear courtyard. One was Mrs. Fergusson's, a new model, long and sleek and green; the next was Mrs. Tafoya's, a drive-yourself Chevy; and the third was the salesman's, a serviceable black business coupe that had seen better days. There was no one and nothing informative in any of them. The outsize sample case in the coupe held exactly what it should have held if Jackson was on the level, a large assortment of bras and girdles carefully wrapped in tissue, and a number of brochures and folders filled with advertising material. There was a soggy chewed-up cigar butt in the ash tray and three or four chewing gum wrappers on the floor, and that was all.

Henry Hilliard's Rolls was parked in the driveway around at the front. It was in immaculate order. The three large bags in the luggage compartment belonged to the girl and Mrs. Mole and Hilliard. They were all initialed and expensive. They weren't locked. They contained clothes carefully packed and nothing else informative.

McKee took the various license numbers and mileages for checking later. It was cold and the air was raw. He pulled his hat brim lower and his slicker collar higher. "Now I want to have a look at that barn again—just to be sure that whoever we disturbed didn't go back and take cover there again after Hilliard and I left." They plodded on through adobe mud that was like glue. Although the rain had stopped, it had done its work as far as the ground underfoot was concerned.

Inside the barn the chill was still bone-piercing in spite of the drop in the wind. The intruder, male or female, had evidently not returned. Gomez's room was just as it had been, the tossed blankets in the same shape as they had been left. A brief glance into the stables beyond; Mary Dane's body had not been disturbed in any way, and the stallion and the black mare were quiet in their stalls. As they started the return journey across the courtyard in the predawn quiet a cock crowed somewhere. There was no faintest gleam in the east, the darkness remained absolute, but morning was not far off now. The sound the cock tossed out triumphantly was loud in the stillness. Water dripped steadily from the branches of the cottonwood tree

as they passed under it, the yellow eye of McKee's flashlight guiding them.

The light picked up something lying close to the tree
trunk, an object that hadn't been there when he and
Hilliard took the same path earlier that night. The Scotsman halted and stooped. It was a rolled newspaper sodden
with moisture. Inside the kitchen with the back door
bolted he examined it. It was yesterday's Albuquerque
Herald.

He said, "Ah—I think our friend, the one who took
refuge in Gomez's bed in the barn, followed Hilliard and
me back here to the house and had a gander through the
window over there to see what was going on. This"—he
tapped the paper—"could have fallen out of his coat pocket
then . . . Let's have a look."

He spread the newspaper flat on the table, and found
what he sought almost at once—the real estate section was
turned out. It was a short folksy item halfway down the
page. "We understand that Rancho El Toro, owned by
the Dane family for well over a century and a half, has
been rented to a couple from the East, Mr. and Mrs.
Fergusson, with an option to buy. Mrs. Fergusson takes
possession today. Mr. Fergusson is settling up his affairs in
the East and will join his wife." A brief summary of the
property and its former glories followed, with the added
statement that Miss Mary Dane was still in the neighborhood staying with friends on a nearby ranch. There was
a check made by a ball point pen in the margin beside the
announcement.

Both men looked at the check. "So whoever was out
there in the barn wasn't there by chance, a drifter taking
cover from the storm?" Steele asked.

"No," McKee said decisively. "Whoever it was is
interested in this place, very much interested—as witness
that check mark . . ."

He rerolled the paper thoughtfully and then proceeded

on to the room down the corridor to relieve the reluctant Ward. He would be glad to see them. The door wasn't locked . . . McKee frowned and threw it open. Ward didn't turn or look around. He didn't move because he couldn't. He was slumped sideway in the chair near the fire where they had left him.

He wasn't dead. His pulse was slow but steady enough. He had been sapped on the back of the head near the base of the skull. The blow he had received hadn't broken the skin but a sizeable lump was forming. McKee stood back and looked around. The picture was easy enough to read. Ward had probably been dozing, his head forward, when he was conked from behind. The blow had been meant to knock him out, not to kill, in order to give whoever struck him time to search the room thoroughly.

The mixture as before, McKee reflected wryly. If at first you don't succeed—on this second occasion the search had been more thorough, and no attempt whatever had been made to conceal it, possibly because of the necessity of hurrying. Also the searcher probably didn't want to be recognized in case Ward should happen to come to. The top of the old chest at the foot of the bed was flung up and its contents tossed about, the desk was open, drawers gaping, and the doors of the wardrobe were wide.

"Will he be all right?" Steele asked, looking pityingly at Ward's young face. McKee said, "I think so, in a couple of hours. That lump seems to me to be too low for a concussion. A thumping headache will be about all, I imagine . . ."

Steele's gaze moved. It went to the door and back to the chair in which Ward was slumped. His eyes and mouth suddenly narrow, Steele said, "You don't suppose someone took Ward for me in this dim light, Inspector?" He waved at the distant lamp.

McKee gave him a sharp sideways glance, while he eased Ward's position. He stood erect, groping in a pocket for a cigarette. "What exactly do you mean by that, Mr. Steele?"

The writer shrugged. "Well, they knew, all these people here, that I was in this room, keeping an eye on Gomez."

The Scotsman studied him. "Have you any reason to suppose that someone now present in this house would want to knock you unconscious, Mr. Steele?" His earlier suspicions of the other man came seeping back.

Steele hesitated, but only for a moment. Mrs. Tafoya had been a witness of his meeting with Rita Mole in the kitchen last night. She might not say anything, she was a bit of a mystery woman herself—but better play it carefully. McKee was an extremely clever man; he was also a police official—and give a dog a bad name . . . Moreover he himself had a job to do and premature disclosure might upset the apple cart. He said, "Have I reason to suspect that anyone here would attack me?"

"That's right, you, personally."

"No, Inspector, I can't really say I have—but after what's happened . . . Don't forget I was in this room when the first searcher entered it, by way of the lumber room and that concealed door over there behind the desk. I was asleep and didn't see anyone, but whoever it was may not be sure of that, and may have wanted to make sure. You say the blow's low, but that might have been accident, Ward might have moved as the weapon came down on his head."

Ingenious, McKee thought, but not the truth—or not all of it. "Mr. Steele, have you ever met any of these people here in the hacienda before?"

Steele said yes.

"Who?"

"Mrs. Mole, and her sister, Miss Sheppard." He held a match to the Scotsman's cigarette, lit one for himself.

"You knew the two women in New York?"

"That's right, I was a friend of Pete Mole's, the lady's late husband."

There was detestation in his tone. McKee continued to study him speculatively. Mrs. Mole and his own first sight of her . . . It was just possible—he tried a shot at random.

"Were you by any chance at the White Queen Hotel in Denver this morning—no, that's not right, yesterday morning?" The shot hit the target, more than that it was a bull's-eye.

Without any hesitation whatever this time Steele said, "I was."

"And did you see Mrs. Mole in the hotel, with her sister and her sister's fiancé?" It might have been the sight of Steele that had sent the large languid mink-coated beauty into a tailspin in the White Queen lobby. That was what might have made her insist on leaving in such a tearing hurry over the objections of Hilliard and her younger sister . . .

Steele was being crowded into a corner. He made up his mind, he had to. His jaw tightened. He tossed his cigarette into what remained of the fire, faced McKee and said quietly, "Inspector, I came out here to the Southwest on business of my own, private business. It has nothing whatever to do with this ranch, or anything that has happened on it since we got here—absolutely nothing, I can assure you of that. I never heard the name Dane in my life before we turned through those gates. I never saw either Veronica or Mary Dane or—that poor fellow, Gomez." He nodded toward the sheeted figure on the bed. "That's all I can tell you at this point, all I can say."

The Scotsman sighed inwardly. But he knew a stone wall when he ran into one. Steele wasn't going to give. There was no doubt about that—and he had no way of making him . . . He contented himself with a warning.

"Mr. Steele, concealing anything in a situation like this,

however extraneous it may seem, is dangerous. We don't know the motive for these crimes, either for the strangling of Mary Dane, or the mortal blow that struck Gomez down, so that no one can positively say what may or may not be important, no matter how irrelevant it may appear to be on the surface."

He paused and looked at Steele. As if to point up his words the vast house gave out vague sounds that were like a long moan in the stillness. It was simply the creaking of old timbers resettling after the departure of the storm, but there was a suggestion of threat in it in the dawn silence, an eerie note. It had no effect whatever on Steele. He repeated firmly, "I can only say that I know nothing, absolutely nothing, about either of these killings and nothing that would throw, could possibly throw, the slightest light on them."

McKee accepted it philosophically. Steele was tough, and resolute, but there were other ways of proceeding . . . Also when Gomez's watch was examined by the experts they could tell whether the hands had been fooled with or not—meanwhile keep things on an even keel. Outside the cock crowed again, more lustily. The windows were getting very faintly gray. Full day wasn't far off.

Ward was still dead to the world, slumped sideway over the chair arm. They made him more comfortable with a pillow behind his head and a blanket around him. The room was cold. Waiting for him to come to, they talked desultorily. McKee said that if Speaker had been able to get through, the police ought to arrive not too long after daylight. Of course, it was a big if.

Steele seemed glad to get away from his own concerns. His manner was easier, more relaxed. "Where do you suppose that fellow who was in Gomez's room in the barn and who followed you as far as the back door has got to?"

McKee shrugged. "Who knows? He may be miles from here by now, he's had plenty of time and nothing to stop him. Somehow or other I doubt it. He may move off a little but I'm pretty sure that he'll be back."

The light continued to grow but not very fast. Frowning, McKee went over to one of the gray windows, stared through the misted panes, and threw the window up sharply. His guess was right. The grayness outside was fog, and it was a heavy one. Its chill damp breath eddied through the opening insidiously in wisps and tatters. He shut the window. It was stiff and he had to use force and it came down with a slam. Fog—it was another form of darkness wiping out all visibility, and they'd had more than enough of that.

The bang of the falling window made Ward stir and his eyes opened. He looked vacantly at the *viga* ceiling for a second or two and then at McKee and Steele. "Where . . . ? What . . . ?" He tried to sit up, winced, and fell back against the pillow. But his eyes stayed open and presently he was able to talk coherently. It didn't do very much good.

Ward didn't know who had hit him or with what. All he knew was that it had felt like a crowbar. "I was sitting here in this chair, I guess I was beginning to fall asleep, when I got it." He admitted guiltily having left the door into the hall a little ajar. "I don't know, I somehow kind of didn't like being shut up in here alone with—with him." He glanced nervously toward the bed. The sheeted figure in it was invisible from where he sat. He said, "He—he didn't come to, did he, and—?"

"No," McKee assured him, "Gomez is dead. It was someone else who slipped in here and gave you that clout over the head. You had no warning, didn't hear any sound at all?" But Ward had heard nothing whatever. One moment he was half asleep, and the next, after that belt, nowhere at all. "Couldn't I—I'd like to get out of here now." He was still uneasy in the presence of death.

There was no reason against it. Gomez was beyond

further attack and the room had already been thoroughly ransacked. McKee said, "If you can walk," and between them he and Steele got Ward up and out of the room and along the corridor, through the empty kitchen, and on into the little room off the pantry. Once safely there Ward relaxed on the narrow bed with a sigh of deep relief. He said, "Thanks," with an attempt at his usual pleasant smile. "My head aches like hell, but I'm glad to be out of there. I sure am."

McKee had another look at his head. The lump at the base of the hair was as big as an egg. "We'll get some compresses on it later, get you some aspirin. Someone must have some. You don't mind staying here alone?" Ward said fervently, "I don't mind anything so long as I'm not with that—that poor stiff shut up in that room. I know it's crazy but at first I kept listening for him to move, for the sheets to rustle and him to get up out of bed . . ."

He gave a lopsided half-ashamed grin. McKee said, "The police ought to be here soon," and the grin wiped itself out.

"The police? . . ." He stared with all his eyes. "But —how? I mean the telephone wires are down and—"

"Mr. Speaker, the rancher who came here looking for Miss Dane, was going to get in touch with them as soon as it got light, or make an almighty try anyhow, and he's much nearer the state barracks."

There was fear in Ward. He tried to conceal it but the freckles stood out on his pallid skin as definitely as ink spots.

"Have you any reason to be afraid of the police, Mr. Ward?" McKee asked.

"No—no," Ward said stammeringly. "No, I haven't. I've never done anything wrong."

The Scotsman didn't believe him. There certainly was something, his agitation was plain. A juvenile misdemeanor perhaps, but Ward was no longer a juvenile. He might be only eighteen or nineteen as he said, but the hard-working life he had led had toughened and matured him . . . His mother had worked for the Danes and while it was a long time ago Mary Dane had kept in touch with her on and off over the years. The murders had been perpetrated here at El Toro, the second to conceal the first, for a time anyhow. And Ward had been attempting to leave the ranch in a hurry when he had run into them early last night and was stopped cold . . . Young he might be and eminently likeable, but at that point no one could be given a clean bill of health.

Steele had gone into the kitchen to make coffee. McKee said, "You'll need cold water for that lump," and left the room, closing the door firmly behind him.

8

He didn't go far. In the middle of the pantry he came to a noiseless halt and stood listening intently. Nothing at first and then there was movement in the room he had just left. The sound was soft, stealthy. He turned quickly back and threw the door wide. Ward was at the room's only window in the act of opening it inch by inch. The ground there was only four or five feet below, an easy drop.

At McKee's entrance he swung around and the window fell with a resounding crash.

Ward's face was paper-white under the freckles. "Some air," he stammered, "it's"—he licked his lips—"it's so stuffy in here."

He wouldn't have deceived a child. There was guilt written all over him. McKee eyed him steadily and kept it up. After a full half-minute had passed he said sternly, "Mr. Ward, don't you think you'd be wiser to come clean? Just now you were trying to get away from this place, a place in which two people have been murdered within the last twelve hours—"

"*Two* people—*two?*" Ward's eyes were big and round and scared.

The Scotsman nodded. "Yes, you heard me the first time. Mary Dane was strangled out there in the barn yesterday in the late afternoon or early evening and her death led to Gomez's."

"*Miss Dane!*"

That got to Ward. He dropped down on the edge of the bed legless and sat there staring blindly at McKee. Sweat sprang out on his forehead. A drop ran down one cheek. He wiped it away with the back of his hand. McKee went on in the same hard tone. "You were trying to make a getaway before the police could possibly arrive."

That did it. Ward broke. He licked his lips again. "I knew it," he said in a low voice, "I always knew it would happen. Bill said the cops would never catch up with us, but I knew he was wrong, I knew they would. Cops never give up."

It came out in bits and pieces. Bill was Ward's older brother, or rather his stepbrother. His stepfather had been married before. Almost five years ago Bill and some of the boys had stolen a car in the late summer—and Ward had tagged along. "If only I'd known what was going to happen—but I was just a crazy kid." He said they hadn't meant to really steal the car, they took it for a joy ride down to Santa Fe for the fiesta there. But they'd had a couple of drinks and on the way down they hit a man walking along the side of the road. He was pretty badly hurt. It sobered the gang up and they turned back and sped off, abandoning the car near the outskirts of Chavez.

Ward wiped his wet forehead again. The man that had been hit died later on. After his death the police had come sniffing around, but Bill made them all swear to button their lips and sit tight, and it had worked. The cops suspected them but they couldn't prove anything. Where was Bill now? He was dead. He had been killed in a car crash himself down in Mexico.

"But I knew that wasn't the finish of it," Ward said

despairingly. "I always knew it. I told Bill so in the beginning but he told me to shut up." Their names had been taken at the time as possible suspects, and if the police found him here in this place . . . "Don't you see? They'll try to pin what happened here on me, I know they will. Once you're in their black books you're sunk."

His despondency and fear were unmistakable. "How old were you when this happened?" McKee asked. He had been almost sixteen, and Bill was nineteen. "Will you—are you going to tell the cops when they come?"

A kid, McKee thought, drawn into an escapade that had turned into a tragedy. But he was under age and he hadn't been driving the death car. "Ever been in any trouble since?" he asked.

"Never. Once was enough," Ward said fervently. "I sure had it. But it will kill Ma if she finds out I was with the gang that night instead of in bed . . ."

The Scotsman took himself away from the wall he was leaning against. "All right—I won't say anything unless it becomes necessary—that is, if you stick around and don't try to take off."

Ward was almost overcome with gratitude and relief. "I won't, Inspector. I promise you I won't. I'll do anything you tell me to do."

He got back under the covers and McKee left the little room. Steele and Ward; backgrounds were beginning to paint themselves in, dimly—how much they were worth or how complete they actually were remained to be seen.

When he went in, the kitchen was big and cold and empty except for the writer who had put a kettle on to boil and built up the fire with fresh logs. He was warming his hands at the infant blaze. Almost full day outside now, it was after half-past six, but the light was poor. McKee went to the back door and opened it. The fog was as thick as ever, a solid gray wall hemming the hacienda in, sealing it off. You couldn't see two feet in front of your nose.

Steele made the coffee expertly. He was evidently a man used to doing things for himself. He had said very little about his circumstances but he was probably either a bachelor, or separated from his wife, and lived alone. Mrs. Fergusson was the first arrival. She came in as McKee and Steele were having a cup at the long center table, after having brought a cup in to Ward with some aspirin from a shelf above the sink.

Mrs. Fergusson was completely dressed, even to the long dangling earrings. Possibly she slept in them. Her penciled eyebrows went up when she saw them. She was shrewd. Seeing them together she guessed. "The yardman?" she asked, and McKee told her.

Her only perceptible emotion at the news of Gomez's death was annoyance. "Hell!" she said succinctly. "But at that I'm not surprised. I didn't think he had a chance when I looked in at him last night . . . It's going to make a lot of trouble. I wanted to get into Albuquerque early today. There are a lot of things I need. Now I suppose we'll have to sit around here and twiddle our thumbs until the police come." She got china out of a cabinet with an ill-tempered rattling and started to prepare her breakfast.

The next arrival was Mrs. Tafoya. Unlike Mrs. Fergusson and her bold movements, she crept into the room. Her hair was more tightly pulled back from her face than ever, giving her a skinned-rabbit effect, a dun-colored rabbit with steel-rimmed glasses that were a little askew. "Gomez dead? . . . Poor man, poor man . . ." Alice-sit-by-the-fire. Steele poured her a cup of coffee and she took it over to her accustomed chair near the hearth with its back to the room.

By seven o'clock there was still no sign of the police. The nothingness surrounding the sprawling house was profound. It not only blanketed the light, it cut off sound. The change from the tumult of the storm of the night before was tremendous but it was no improvement. Lamps had to be lit. With nothing to do but wait, McKee was at a loose end. Steele, too, was restless. From time to time he kept glancing at Mrs. Tafoya's averted face. The Scotsman wondered what he was going to say or do when Mrs. Mole and the Sheppard girl eventually appeared, and went in and took a look at young Ward.

Ward was asleep and McKee wandered to the front of the house. Odd about the nonarrival of some official. Speaker looked like a dependable man and he had said come hell or high water he'd get word to the police at the crack of dawn. That was well over two hours ago. Surely someone should have appeared by this time if he had managed to get through to the state barracks, and Albuquerque was only twenty miles away on the floor of the valley to the west. True the wires were down, but there must be some sort of local official here in a township or county in the lower Sandias, a sheriff or some such. Maybe Speaker hadn't been able to inform anyone . . .

The thought of being marooned here indefinitely was not a pleasant one . . . Presently he went outside. The visibility hadn't improved in the slightest in any direction. He sauntered around the house to make sure. The air, wet as it was, was faintly warmer, but the fog was as thick as ever. There was no break in it anywhere. He kept close to the walls. Uneasiness pervaded him. Perhaps Speaker might have been hurt getting home, might be lying somewhere out in the open with a broken leg . . . More than once he cursed James Ringrose for the scenic short cut he had advised over the phone. Trying to follow it was what had got him into this mess here—and it was a very thorough mess indeed.

In the courtyard at the back of the hacienda he almost ran into someone. It was Mrs. Tafoya in an old slicker that was too big for her carrying a pail loaded with scraps for the chickens. "I thought they—they might be hungry, you know." Her mousy brown hair was beaded with drops of moisture. She blinked at him owlishly, she had taken her glasses off. She was probably country-bred, he decided, watching her pick a careful way through the mud under the cottonwood branches. After a few steps the fog swallowed her up.

It was a fog and a half and then some. In his inattention McKee lost contact with the house and fetched up under the portal on the far side of the courtyard. There was a car close to him. It was Mrs. Tafoya's rented Chevy. He peered right and left. Mrs. Fergusson's long sleek job was there—but Jackson's old business coupe was not. It was gone.

Gazing at the space where it had stood he whistled softly to himself. Well, well, not an adventurous fellow, Mr. Jackson, from the look of him, definitely no. And yet he had taken off at an unknown hour during the night that was past under what were practically suicidal conditions . . . Very interesting. Perhaps someone had heard him go. McKee found his way to the back door and went inside. The shadowy kitchen was empty. He walked through it and on into the dining room, and came to a halt just short of the living-room archway.

There were people in there, a man and a woman. The man was Steele, the woman was Hilliard's fiancée, Jill Sheppard. They weren't within his field of vision but he could see them plainly, or rather their reflections, in a long mirror on the wall over the old-fashioned grand piano.

Jill Sheppard was standing on the stairs, three steps from the bottom, one hand on the banister railing. She was holding herself very erect, shoulders back, her head high. Her small face was bleak. Red mouth bunched, she was looking down at Steele a few yards away, below her. Evidently in answer to a query of his she said, "Oh, yes, I knew you were here in this house, that you came with that inspector—rather odd company for you, wasn't it? Rita told me you were here, that she saw you last night.

Poor thing, she was terribly nervous and upset and who could blame her? What I'd like to know is how dared you follow us out here—how *dared* you?—after what you did. Or wasn't it enough for you? What more do you want, what are you after?"

Her voice had a lash to it. Steele seemed unaffected, he remained perfectly controlled. He said coolly, "What am I after? That's easy. I want the truth. If you'll listen to me for just a moment—"

Jill Sheppard brushed that aside. "The truth," she cried scornfully, "the truth, the truth—everyone knows the truth about you. You tried to lie out of it—to . . ." Anger choked her.

Steele put a match to his cigarette. "My dear girl— that's where you're wrong. You ought to get your facts straight. You really ought. Or don't you want to know the facts? Perhaps you're afraid that this—this new man of yours, this stuffed shirt you're engaged to, wouldn't like it. He's rich, isn't he? . . . I never knew you were so fond of money, tarred with the same brush as that sister of yours. Oh well, live and learn. It's all part of the ball game."

He could hit back, and did. His own gibing tone had a savage bite to it. The girl's eyes blazed down at him. She was rigid with rage. "Don't you *dare* say anything about Henry. I've known Henry all my life—and I love him and I trust him . . ."

"Now isn't that nice? Just the way it should be. Idyllic. Let's hope it will only continue. But fidelity's not one of your particular virtues, is it?"

A voice from the floor above, calling the girl's name; it sounded like Rita Mole. Jill Sheppard turned. She said, flinging the words contemptuously over her shoulder, "Fidelity?—not that kind, not when it's founded on sand," and ran quickly up the stairs. Steele remained where he was, looking after her.

McKee watched him absently in the mirror. The story

was easy enough to read, the general outlines of it. Steele had been mixed up with the girl emotionally in some way. Perhaps she had even been going to marry him, or he thought so. At any rate, egged on by her older sister she had evidently broken it off and was now engaged to Henry Hilliard . . . He walked on into the living room.

Steele corroborated his guess when he apologized for being in the next room and overhearing.

"Think nothing of it," he said, "lots of people know. Yes, six months ago I thought Miss Sheppard was going to do me the honor of becoming my lawfully wedded wife, with bell, book and candle and a white veil. All the trimmings. But she changed her mind. Women often do when something better comes along."

"And you followed her west, followed the Rolls from Denver down here to try and make her change her mind back again?"

Steele tapped a cigarette on the back of a lean hand. "I don't know about changing her mind . . . I certainly wanted to talk to her—alone. I also wanted to talk to the charming Mrs. Mole. But I lost the Rolls when we started to climb into these mountains, quite a while before my car ditched itself and I ran into you. I didn't know, hadn't the slightest idea that—eh—Mr. Hilliard and party had taken refuge in this damn place. All I do know is that I'll be glad to get out of it." He looked at his watch. "It's almost eight o'clock. Where in hell are the police?"

It was a straight story as far as it went and Steele's love life was his own . . . A blur of voices on the floor above, doors closing. Rita Mole said, "Wouldn't it be a good idea to take the bags down now so that we'll be ready to leave?" Hilliard answered her. "Time enough after we've had coffee," he said. "Sleep well, Jill? You look rather tired."

McKee stopped listening at that point. What made him stop was a cry from somewhere outside the hacienda.

It was faint, muffled. It sounded like a call for help. He crossed to the front door in a hurry and pulled it open. Gray billows of fog pushed at him wetly. The fog wasn't as stationary as it had been earlier, a low wind had sprung up. He advanced to the edge of the paved terrace. It was three or four feet above ground level. Out in front the fog was parting here and there in places. It eddied away, eddied back. Now the half-strangled cries were nearer, and louder. Steele had joined McKee.

"Look. Over there." Beside the Scotsman, Steele pointed to the south. A channel had opened up there. It was walled with fog. What they saw at the end of it was a man swimming. His head was just above water. Then the fog closed in again.

9

The swimmer was the salesman, Jackson. They got to him in time. The moment they leaped down from the terrace they were waist-high in water, then it was shoulder-high and deepening, and they had to swim themselves, guided by Jackson's voice. The salesman had all but had it when they reached him. Flood waters covered the whole valley floor. Between them they got him safely back to the hacienda which stood on slightly higher ground.

Three-quarters of an hour later, in a bathrobe of Hilliard's and with a blanket around him, Jackson talked in the now crowded kitchen, partially revived by a large whiskey after the water was out of his lungs. Glass in hand he told them what had happened to him. He said that he hadn't been able to sleep much during the night and when the rain stopped toward morning he decided to beat it out of there and get an early start down to Albuquerque. The light wasn't very good and at first he didn't see much water because of the fog. He figured there was only a couple of feet of it, that he'd soon be through that. Then there was more and then more water and it was all about him and the car was getting in deeper and deeper. He didn't know how he had managed to get the door partially open; anyway, he said, he dived through it.

"I knew I'd be trapped inside the car if I didn't and that'd be the end of me. Curtains." He couldn't see where he was going because of the fog. He had hit his head against something he later discovered to be a tree. He clung to it for a while, then he began to get really scared. The water was rising higher by the minute. As the light grew he saw he was near the driveway leading to the hacienda. He knew his only hope was to swim for it, there was nothing else to do. He shivered at the memory.

"I'm not much of a swimmer. The old breast stroke . . . But I kept on and I yelled, and kept on yelling." Jackson swallowed the rest of his drink in a gulp.

McKee, Steele and Hilliard had already made an exploratory tour. What Jackson said was true. The hacienda was completely surrounded by water. The fog was thinning but the water was rising slowly but steadily. There was no escape route. It was now plain why the police hadn't arrived. Granting, that was, that the rancher had been able to notify them, they couldn't get through. The night before Speaker had been afraid that Chavez Creek would overflow its banks, swollen to immense proportions by the tons of water pouring down into it from the rushing arroyos, and that was what had evidently happened. The whole narrow valley must be under water. Hilliard, who knew the topography, didn't think there was any real danger, or not immediately at any rate. They might ultimately have to retreat to the second floor or even the roof, but he doubted whether the flood waters would rise higher than that. Of course, there was always a chance of it. Back in the kitchen they said nothing of this to the women.

When Jackson finished talking Rita Mole gathered folds of mink closer about her in her chair near the hearth.

"I was hoping we could get away, that we'd be gone by now. This terrible place." She shuddered and waved a hand that took in the desolation outside. Jackson eyed the two handsome rings on her white fingers. His agreement was heartfelt. "You ain't kidding, lady." Nobody else said anything. Mrs. Fergusson and Mrs. Tafoya were at opposite windows looking out into the grayness of fog close to the panes.

McKee roused himself. He said that the first thing to do was to replenish the supplies in the hacienda, get in all the wood they could before the water in the rear courtyard, now a foot deep, rose any higher. The next—"What about food, Mrs. Fergusson?"

Nothing could apparently disturb their involuntary hostess's stony composure and in some odd way the flood cutting them off from the outside world appeared to be not unpleasant to her. She said there was enough for a couple of days, and there was more meat in one of the outbuildings, more hams and bacon and some deer meat.

Another outburst from Mrs. Mole. A couple of days —she refused to believe it. Surely someone would come, help would arrive soon, in a matter of three or four hours at the most. It *had* to.

Hilliard's patience with his prospective sister-in-law was wearing thin. He said help would arrive eventually but it might take time and meanwhile they'd all have to put up with it. They could be a lot worse off, stranded in a car for instance without any food. Rita Mole seemed to be a little afraid of him and she subsided, which was all to the good. Hysteria, panic, were catching, and she was on the edge of it. They had all accepted the yardman's death apathetically. With the exception of Hilliard, Steele and Ward, none of the others knew about Mary Dane lying out there in the barn, and what had happened to her.

It was at that point that young Ward came into the kitchen—and the fat was in the fire. Ward was still more than a bit groggy. "The flood," he said excitedly, "a dead chicken, it just went by my window . . . What about the horses, and that poor dead Miss Dane out there in the stable?"

That did it for fair. A muted scream from Mrs. Mole, raised voices, questions; McKee told them, calmly and curtly, of the finding of Mary Dane's body in the loose box the night before. He was interrupted by Rita Mole.

"That man," she all but screamed, pointing, "that man over there, *he* doesn't mind killing people, he killed my husband . . ."

She was pointing at Steele, leaning at ease against the far wall, hands in his pockets.

Steele didn't even bother to straighten up. He merely smiled. "Your husband died of a heart attack, Mrs. Mole, and you know it."

"A heart attack, yes," she cried, "but what brought it on?"

Startled and curious glances going from one to the other; McKee was interested himself but this was neither the time nor the place. He cut in coldly.

"Mrs. Mole, Mr. Steele had nothing whatever to do with Miss Dane's death. I can assure you, all of you, of that. The yardman was struck down shortly after Mary Dane died, and Mr. Steele was with me, some distance from this house, when she was killed."

Rita Mole's mouth snapped shut in a dead white face. She didn't seem to believe him, but it stopped her for the moment anyhow and he went on. Offer them a victim, someone not in the hacienda now they could concentrate on. He said that a man had been hiding in the barn when he and Hilliard discovered Miss Dane's body. This man was gone. From the look of things he appeared to have made his escape from El Toro before the water began to rise and was probably miles away by now. But the police would catch up with him eventually.

More babble, more questions, but the momentary excitement raised by Mrs. Mole's point-blank accusation of one of their number had subsided, and they were all quieter. McKee registered various impressions. There was relief of some sort in Mrs. Fergusson behind her cast-iron front. In Jackson, too? No break in Mrs. Tafoya's aloofness where she stood at one of the windows with her back to the room. And there had been a change in the girl, too. Jill Sheppard's antagonism toward Steele was still in her, but it appeared to have abated slightly. She had flinched when her sister made her bald accusation, had cast several covert glances at him since as though some certainty in her had weakened . . . He filed these things for reference later; at the moment there was plenty of work to do.

The water in the courtyard went on rising steadily. It was up to the floorboards of the various cars before noon. But by that time almost all the available wood had been carried in and stored in the scullery and the oil tanks pretty well emptied of their contents into every available container. Also more meat, a haunch of frozen venison, three hams and some flitches of bacon—Mrs. Fergusson had given the Scotsman the key to the padlock of the cold room—had been stored in the pantry.

Extra chairs had also been brought into the kitchen. Except for a little moving about at intervals they all remained there, a wretched and for the most part silent congregation of strangers and pilgrims. Rita Mole had tentatively proposed a fire in the small room off the dining room at the front of the hacienda but when Hilliard negatived that—"We can't spare any extra logs, Rita," she had submitted meekly enough. "I suppose not, Henry, whatever you say."

Lunch, a scratch lunch, was set out on the long table by Mrs. Fergusson and Mrs. Tafoya. Jill Sheppard helped. The useless phone, the creeping flood outside under the leaden sky—the body of the yardman in the late Veronica

Dane's bedroom and her sister's, lying outside in the stables alone in the chill, although not much more was said about them, were a crushing pall. The general mood was that if only they knew what was happening, what was likely to happen—but they were as cut off from the world as though they were on the moon.

At shortly after two o'clock, putting down an empty coffee cup, Hilliard struck his forehead with an open palm. "Bone, solid bone and nothing but—what a fool I am not to have thought of it before." He pushed back his chair. There was a transistor radio in the glove compartment of the Rolls. "We can at least get some news—if it isn't too late, if the water hasn't gotten to the batteries."

Steele in hip boots and a slicker had just come in with a final few logs. He said, "I've got these things on anyhow. If you'll give me your keys I'll go and get it."

He came back with the radio. He had been only just in time. The water had almost reached the glove compartment. He handed the radio to Hilliard. Hilliard took it out of its leather case and adjusted dials.

The voice, a strange voice from the outside world, was a shock in the big waiting shadowy room surrounded by mountains, and miles from anywhere. The news from KGGM in Albuquerque was certainly not good. Most of it was concerned with the storm. They all listened intently.

The announcer said that it had created havoc over practically the whole state. There were floods everywhere and bridges were down, and a lot of roads washed out. There were eight known dead, the toll would probably be much higher . . . People were requested to open their houses to the occupants of stranded cars in their neighborhood. The storm was not yet over . . . A mass of cold air was moving down from the north. Snow was expected that night in the higher mountain valleys, rain below the four-thousand-foot line . . . Communications were disrupted and a number of places were completely cut off. A scarcity of men . . . Many communities without light or heat, emergency crews working . . .

It was obvious to everyone there that the prospect of rescue immediately, in a matter of a few hours or so, was so remote as to be practically nonexistent. There they were and there they were stuck. Hilliard switched off the radio and the silence inside and out came back. It was gloomy, oppressive. Rita Mole was crushed, sat with a hand across her eyes. No one had any comment to make except Hilliard himself.

He said easily, "These announcer fellows are all alarmists, like to make a thing of their reports . . . It's probably not half as bad as he paints it . . ." Jackson responded valiantly. He was the only one who did. "Sure, sure . . . Anyways, what are we kicking about, folks? We got a roof over our heads, haven't we, and the fire to keep us nice and cozy and plenty to eat and drink? Me, I'm satisfied."

Steele walked out of the kitchen. Presently McKee followed him. He found the writer in the dining room pacing the floor. "Nice view out there. Pretty," Steele said and waved toward the windows. His tone was grim, his expression savage.

The view was rather appalling now that the fog, except for bits and pieces here and there, had almost entirely cleared off. Mountains tumbled up into the sky, high, bleak, saw-toothed and cruel, peak after peak from every window in sight. They hemmed in the narrow inundated valley, a mere slit not at the most more than half a mile wide, seemed to bend over it . . . At the moment the Scotsman's interest was more immediately engaged. He parked himself on a corner of the long table.

"Mr. Steele—what did Mrs. Mole mean when she accused you of killing her husband a few minutes ago?"

Steele sat down on a high carved chair and took out a

cigarette. He thought for a moment or two, then he shrugged. "What the hell . . . I suppose you might as well have it now as later." He began to talk.

He and Pete Mole, Rita Mole's husband and a friend of his, had worked together for a while in the same office in an investment house in New York. Mole was his boss, Steele just a part-time assistant, a leg man, doing his own work, his writing, on the side. The job didn't pay much but it eked out his income, and much more important, gave him the background for the book he was then engaged on. Mission accomplished; he finished the book and decided to leave, but Pete Mole had asked him to stay on for another month and to please Pete he had agreed.

It was during his last week with the firm that it happened. Twenty thousand dollars in cash was stolen from the safe in Pete Mole's office.

"Twenty thousand—"

"That's right, Inspector." Steele said that the twenty thousand, from the sale of bonds belonging to a woman client, was to have been handed over to her on the following day.

He got out of the chair and began to walk up and down the floor again. "Sure I knew the combination of the safe, and sure I went back to the office that night after everyone had gone. What I went back for was some notes I'd left in my desk, but would anyone believe that? Not on your life."

He thrust a fresh cigarette between his lips. The flame of the match was bright in the icy chill of the bleak room. "There was a crude attempt to make it look like an outside job. The door of the fire stairs was supposed to have been propped open, a piece of wood was found on the landing, and a couple of the drawers of Pete Mole's desk were pulled out and papers were messed up. The police were called in.

"Besides the senior vice-president, and he was in Florida, only Pete and I knew the combination of the safe. As far as the firm went Pete Mole was above suspicion, he had been with them for more than twenty years. So," Steele shrugged, "I was tagged it. Luckily I have a friend who also happens to be a smart lawyer. The D.A.'s office tried to get an indictment against me. No soap. Insufficient evidence —case dismissed. That's the story." McKee looked at him.

"It doesn't explain why Mrs. Mole said you'd killed her husband."

Steele was offhand. "Pure invention on her part. And spite. Pete felt responsible I suppose, he had hired me and he worried a lot . . . A month or so after it was all over he had a fatal heart attack."

"And after his death Miss Sheppard—"

"Gave me the heave ho. She was very fond of Pete."

It might be the story, but it wasn't the whole story; McKee kept after Steele. Driven into a corner he finally came clean, but only after the Scotsman assured him that the case was of no interest to him professionally no matter what had happened.

Steele said, "Yes, I know Pete had done it, and I know why. The poor old guy needed the money for that blood-sucking cormorant of a wife of his. Talk of someone killing him—she was the one . . . After his heart attack he lived on for a couple of weeks and before he died he wrote me a letter. I suppose he got one of the nurses to post it for him. I didn't get it until around Christmas, I was out of New York. Anyhow, when I got Pete's letter I tried to see Miss Sheppard, but she had come west with her sister, and was already tied up with Hilliard. I didn't give a damn about that but I made up my mind both she and her sister were going to read Pete's letter."

"You have Mr. Mole's letter with you?" McKee asked and Steele took it from an inside pocket and handed it to him. The letter was incoherent and rambling, but its import was plain enough. Whether it would stand up in court was something else again. Tough on Steele either way but he was telling the truth. He handed the letter back to the writer and crossed to the window.

What was to be seen of the immediate valley from there was a lake with big trees growing out of it, water halfway up their trunks, and the tops of clumps of smaller trees, feathery tamarisks and Russian olives. Thirty feet to the left was the archway to the rear courtyard with the barn and stables beyond it. Straight ahead water lapped gently against the wire fencing of the corral.

The only thing that moved in the gray desolation were some crows inside the corral, five or six black shapes moving around agitatedly, swooping down, flying off in tight circles, descending again. McKee craned. There was something here, some floating object . . . The hair at the nape of his neck stirred gently. Crows. Carrion crows . . .

Three minutes later in boots and slickers he and Steele were outside and through the corral gates . . . The floating thing behind the stables was not human . . . It was the body of a dog, a black and white dog. A Dalmatian. It was the dog Spot Veronica Dane was holding by the collar in the photograph at the far end of the house. The dog's collar was still on and the metal tag fastened to it was inscribed Spot, V. Dane, El Toro. McKee stooped and examined the dog's body. He didn't have far to look. Spot hadn't died a natural death. He had been shot between the eyes.

He stood erect. "Killed," he said aloud, "at or about the time Veronica Dane died. Must have been hastily and shallowly buried somewhere here in the corral. Water washed the earth away and the body floated."

"*Veronica* Dane?" Steele was puzzled at the intrusion of her name. "Did you say Veronica?"

McKee nodded. "I did."

"Don't you mean Mary?"

"I do not. Mary Dane died less than twenty hours ago. This poor brute has been dead for some time and Veronica

Dane died, suddenly, here in the hacienda a little over four weeks ago . . . I'm beginning to seriously doubt that she died a natural death . . . It's quite possible that she was killed and this"—he waved at the lifeless carcass awash at their feet—"saw the killer, followed him giving tongue and got a bullet through the head."

Steele was utterly out of his depth. He gave his own head a shake. "In God's name, what devil's cauldron have we fallen into?"

"Not a pleasant one certainly—but on the whole simple enough." The Scotsman continued to think aloud. "Veronica Dane wasn't shot, or it would have been discovered at the time . . . Perhaps strangled, or even frightened to death . . . She was supposedly alone in the hacienda. Her sister Mary was shopping in Albuquerque and the cook and Gomez had been given the day off and had gone to a fiesta somewhere . . . The point is that Veronica *wasn't* alone while they were all away. When Mary got back from Albuquerque she found her sister dead in there in her chair at the dining-room table. Her own arrival probably scared the killer off in a hurry before he or she had accomplished his full purpose."

He gazed at the hovering crows scared off momentarily but waiting. "Look at the facts, the searching of Veronica Dane's room *twice* in the last twenty-four hours, the attack on young Ward . . . There's something in this house that someone wants, badly. It could be the thing Mary Dane forgot when she left here with Speaker and came back for yesterday afternoon . . ."

The two men left the corral and waded back to the hacienda. It was colder. A chill wind that had sprung up blew persistently from the east. The tops of the mountains on all sides were veiled. The veils were snow. As they neared the house walls the first flakes came drifting lazily down.

10

McKee and Steele reëntered the haci-
enda by the rear door. In the big shadowy kitchen beyond
the entry Jackson was talking expansively. He was holding
forth on girdles, standing on the hearth smoking a cigar.

"Now you take a good form-fitting support—it doesn't
show on the outside and that's what matters. It's all in the
undergarment, see, how you're shaped and supported.
That's the whole secret. I don't care what kind of a figger
a woman's got, a good girdle'll make it over. It gives her
poise, see, and poise gives her carriage, and that's more than
half the battle. Yes, sir, she knows she looks good, and she
shows it. Now you take that Mrs. Tafoya, for instance;
why I could make her over, make her into a new woman
with one of our Dolly Vardens, five-way stretch, with good
strong bones . . ."

He was apparently talking to Mrs. Mole who sat in a
chair at the other end of the hearth, her mink coat draped
over her shoulders. He might have been addressing himself
to a statue for all the attention she gave him. She was
staring steadily into the flames, a hand shading her eyes.

From her expression the thoughts in which she was immersed didn't appear to be particularly pleasant. The only other one in the big room was Mrs. Fergusson, majestically erect, drying dishes at the drainboard, her earrings swinging with her energetic movements. As the two men came in bringing coldness with them she said curtly over her shoulder, "Shut that door."

Jackson turned quickly at their entrance. His monstrous shadow thrown on the wall followed him in clear outline. McKee's brows went up. Mr. Jackson was wearing a money belt. The bathrobe he had on, which he had borrowed from Hilliard while his own clothes dried, parted for a moment over a well-rounded belly. He retied the robe hurriedly, but not before the edge of the belt showed above a pair of brilliantly striped shorts.

He said cheerfully, rubbing his hands together and beaming, "Been out for a look-see have you, Inspector? Water going down some, I hope?" McKee said no, if anything it was still rising, and asked where the others were. Hilliard and Miss Sheppard were taking a brisk promenade through the rooms at the front to stretch their legs, Ward had a bad headache and had taken more aspirin and gone to lie down, and Mrs. Tafoya was outside having a look at the chickens.

Outside—the woman could have seen and heard what had passed in the corral . . . But it wasn't important, didn't matter really, because in any case it was time now for a showdown. The Scotsman described the discovery of the Dalmatian's body in the corral, flushed from a shallow grave to the surface by the floods. Hilliard and Jill Sheppard came in while he was talking. Iron man as Hilliard was and as an executive used to schooling his expression and bearing as a matter of course, he looked tired, there were new lines in his face, around his mouth and eyes. The girl's eyes were extraordinarily bright and she had more color in her cheeks than usual. Had they perhaps been having words?

The same thought was in Mrs. Mole, she gave both of them a sharp glance.

Hilliard exclaimed at the mention of the Dalmatian. "Veronica's dog, Spot?" His hands tightened on the back of the chair near the fire he held for the girl. At the sink Mrs. Fergusson put down a plate with a clatter and swung around. "Spot, did you say? That's the dog Miss Dane was worried about when she left here with that fellow Speaker. She said the animal disappeared the day her sister died and hadn't appeared since, and asked me to let her know if he turned up here." Mrs. Mole couldn't possibly have been more uninterested in the fate of the animal until McKee said Spot had been shot. Then her white and gold impassivity gave way. "Shot," she cried on a rising note, and pressed a handkerchief to her lips.

"Yes, Mrs. Mole, that's right. Shot."

And that brought the Scotsman to his point. And the point was guns. He wanted to know how many of them had weapons. Starting to light a cigarette Hilliard stopped abruptly. His gaze at McKee was cold, and shrewd.

"Veronica died a natural death almost a month ago, Inspector. Surely you don't think that what happened here yesterday has anything to do with her or with her dog either."

McKee remained affable. He said mildly, "Mr. Hilliard, at this stage I'm not doing any thinking. That's for the New Mexican police when they finally manage to get here. Meanwhile we have to try and collect the facts as best we can."

The only people in the house who owned guns, or at least admitted that they did, were Hilliard and Jackson. Jackson's was in his car under water, a quarter of a mile away. Hilliard's was in the glove compartment of the Rolls, and also probably under water by now. Jackson sometimes carried money, the firm's money—". . . and what I always say with all this crime around and holdups—better be sure than sorry. An ounce of prevention—that's the ticket—yes, sir."

Hilliard said, "For the matter of that, Inspector—come to think of it—there are, or at least there ought to be, some weapons in this house. Veronica used to do a good deal of hunting and some target shooting to keep her hand in. She was a crack shot."

McKee nodded. "If you'll all kindly remain here for a few minutes I'll go and have a look around." He had already spoken to Steele and Steele stayed where he was, in a chair at the table, its back to the group at the fireplace. He hadn't once glanced at Mrs. Mole, or at the girl either since coming in. Hilliard favored McKee's request with a long stare. There was a faint quizzical smile in the tail of it, but he made no open protest and the Scotsman left the room.

If the kitchen was gloomy even in lamp and firelight, the rest of the house was darker still. Snow was driving past the windows. It made no impression on the surface of the steel-colored lake that would shortly be lapping the base of the walls, but whiteness was already beginning to pile up in the corners of the glass panes and the chill was sepulchral. McKee went through room after room on the first floor. There were no guns on the walls or in any of the painted chests. Odd. Country people generally took care of their weapons and were proud of them and they were kept in an accessible place where they could be oiled and cleaned.

Upstairs the first room he entered was Mrs. Tafoya's. Her suitcase, a cheap affair of eighteen carat pasteboard with a slick of varnish over it, was pushed under the neatly made bed. The case was locked, but a knee and a little pressure sprang the flimsy catch. There was no gun in it, but there was something else that held McKee's attention.

Under a long flannelette nightgown, a pair of stockings and a well-worn slip, there was a small bottle of make-up, another labelless bottle of some thick dark liquid, a black grease pencil and a second pair of glasses in one of the bag's side pockets.

McKee put the glasses to his eyes and instantly the room blurred. He took them off thoughtfully, stood swinging them to and fro and nodded. No wonder Mrs. Tafoya had that odd peering look, that forward carriage of the head. The glasses were cheap uncorrected magnifying glasses sold in five-and-ten-cent stores all over the country . . .

He turned his attention to the bottles, the dark oily make-up, and the labelless bottle. The liquid in it was a dye or tint, a smear of it on the back of his hand made a dull brownish stain . . . Well, well—a disguise of sorts. Whatever else the lady was he was willing to hazard a guess that she was not Mrs. Tafoya the drudge, unassuming and quiet, courting no attention, keeping almost humbly apart, keeping to herself. She might have her own reasons for this masquerade. They might be reasons that had nothing to do with her turning up here at El Toro like the others, a stranded traveler, caught by the storm and seeking temporary refuge before getting on to another destination. Might—and might not. She could have come here deliberately, for a definite purpose . . . In any case she would certainly bear close watching.

What else was there? She had been brought up in the country, and she was fond of animals, she had had no difficulty finding her way to the hen house with scraps. She had shown genuine emotion at the first sight of Gomez when he was carried through the kitchen and put into the bed in the room that had been Veronica Dane's when she was alive. And it was a room which had been later entered secretly on two occasions in the night that was past by one of six people . . .

Six people, he thought morosely, six of them if you excluded Steele, to try and keep an eye on, keep from doing any further mischief. And that was leaving out the man in the barn who had been in Albuquerque the day before Mary Dane and Gomez were killed and who had fled the ranch, or apparently fled it, after the discovery of Mary's body in the stallion's loose box.

The wind was rising again, whipping the snow coming down beyond the window sideways, and the light was dimming. He roused himself. Finish up here and then make another and more intensive search of the various outbuildings before darkness came, which wouldn't be long now. McKee replaced the make-up kit under the flannelette nightgown where it had been, put the glasses back in the side pocket, refastened the bag, pushed it back under the bed, left the room and went through Mrs. Mole's, her sister's and Hilliard's in turn. There were no guns and nothing in any of them there shouldn't be.

Of all those uninvited guests, Hilliard and Rita Mole and Jill Sheppard were the most understandable. There was no mystery about them. They were on their way to Hilliard's father's ranch some seven or eight miles off and had had to turn back when they were stopped cold by the bridge that was down across the river to the east. Hilliard knew this house, knew the former occupants, and that they could find shelter here for the night. Mrs. Fergusson's presence also needed no explanation. She had rented El Toro, had taken possession from Mary Dane and was already in residence. That left Jackson and Ward and Mrs. Tafoya. The three of them were necessarily question marks. They could be exactly what they seemed to the outward eye, or the converse. With the ranch in these wild mountains cut off from the outside world and the phone out of commission, there was no possible way of checking on any of their stories.

McKee proceeded to have a look through Jackson's room but it was as bare as a bone—all the salesman's personal belongings were in his submerged car under water halfway to the gates. Where *could* Veronica Dane's guns be? Guns were not only valuable in themselves, they were both fresh meat and security to people living out in the wilds. They were not in the lumber room, he had already gone over it.

About to open the door the Scotsman stood still. Another sound against the swish of the snow. Footsteps were advancing along the corridor. They grew more definite. It was Rita Mole with her sister. They halted near the closed door. Mrs. Mole said, "But why *didn't* you agree, Jill? Naturally Henry would like to have a definite date set. He has a lot of things on his hands, he's an important man—"

"And I, Rita, am an important woman, at least to myself anyhow—something that possibly you've overlooked?"

The girl's voice was cool but Rita Mole was not sensitive to shades; either that or her way of dealing with opposition was to ignore it. A steam roller, McKee thought, a large blonde one not basically unlike the late Veronica Dane . . . She went on plaintively, "Well, I can't understand you, Jill, I really can't. Up until the last few days everything was all right, you seemed content, happy, and I was happy for you, happy that you were so well settled— and now—it can't be that the sight of that horrible man, Steele, that thief and murderer . . ."

Jill Sheppard interrupted her. She said shortly, "Do you want to go into the bathroom, Rita, or did you bring me up here to talk? If you did it's useless. You may as well save your breath."

"Oh, Jill—how can you speak like that? You're the one I'm thinking of but you're so hard . . ."

They moved off. The door to the bathroom at the end of the hall closed. McKee went downstairs. The emotional mix-ups between the girl and her sister and Steele and Hilliard were beyond him, out of his ken, none of his business. What continued to concern him was the whereabouts of the late Veronica's weapons, and more important —the thing Mary Dane had returned to the ranch to get and in doing so had met with a brutal death. Whatever she had come back for must still be here in the hacienda. She didn't appear to have been a careless woman and she would scarcely have left something of value in the stables or barn. Moreover, when she joined Speaker that morning she had come directly out of the house, and not from any of the outbuildings. He went on into the kitchen.

It was warm, the only place of refuge from the bitter chill that pervaded the rest of the hacienda. Flies in amber —same setup. Impassive faces, unreadable. No telling what was going on behind them. Of the women Mrs. Fergusson was the only one there. Rita Mole and her sister were upstairs, McKee knew, but where was Mrs. Tafoya? She hadn't come in from her trip to the hen house. With the entire valley flooded and impassible, even if she wanted to take a powder she couldn't get far. Nevertheless uneasiness stirred in him. She had been out quite a while . . . He said to Steele who had found a book somewhere and was turning the pages idly, "Would you mind going out and having a look around for Mrs. Tafoya?" and Steele got up with alacrity.

"Locate Veronica's guns, Inspector?" Hilliard asked, looking up from a game of solitaire. McKee shook his head. "Not a whiff of them. Nothing."

Leaning against the drainboard, smoking a cigarette, Mrs. Fergusson said suddenly, "I've been thinking about that closet Miss Dane left some things of hers in. She said she'd be back to get them later on. She might have put the guns there. It's locked though, and I have no key. She kept that."

McKee asked, "The closet in the dining room beyond the clock?" Mrs. Fergusson nodded and he retraced his steps.

Mrs. Fergusson was wrong. The closet in the dim

dining room wasn't locked now. The knob turned readily under his hand. He examined the lock. It showed no signs of having been tampered with, nor had the door been forced. He opened it wide. The closet ran back to a depth of less than two feet. It was long and narrow with rows of shelves on either side. The guns were there, neatly arrayed on one of the shelves, two rifles, a shotgun and a revolver. One of them could have been removed of course . . . But there was no possible way to check that.

Hilliard, who had followed him into the dining room, couldn't say exactly how many guns Veronica had had. He recognized one of the rifles and the shotgun which had been her father's. For the rest there were a few treasures— family stuff, a little old china and glassware, several pieces of thin, very ancient old silver, a christening mug holding toothpicks and engraved with the name Charles, and a flat box of polished dark wood.

McKee opened the box. It was empty. But there had been something in it until a short time ago. An oblong on the bottom, five inches wide by about ten long, was dustless on a surrounding field of dust, faint but there.

McKee stood in such a position that Hilliard couldn't see past him. "Anything, Inspector?" he asked.

"Just the guns, and some odds and ends." The Scotsman closed the box thoughtfully. Yes, until very recently, probably twenty-four to thirty-six hours or so, the box which appeared to be ebony had held some object. The thing Mary Dane had forgotten and come back to the hacienda to get? Quite possibly. But at any rate it was gone now. He picked up the silver mug.

"Do you know who Charles is?" he asked.

"Oh yes." Hilliard explained that Charles had been Veronica and Mary's younger brother. He and Veronica had never got along very well, they rubbed each other the wrong way from the time they were kids. And when, after his father's death, Charles brought his wife and child back home to El Toro because he couldn't make a living for them, Veronica had been in a tearing fury. He was a harem-scarem happy-go-lucky lad and he had married imprudently while he was still in college. He and his wife and child had lived at the ranch for some years, two or three at least, and then Charles and his wife took off leaving the child, a girl, with her two aunts for what Charles said would be a month or so. But the month had lengthened into a number of years.

What finally happened to Charles and his wife and the daughter? Hilliard couldn't say. Snow driving softly past the windows; the chill was deeper. Hilliard turned up his coat collar and thrust his hands into his pockets. It seemed to him that he had heard somewhere that the girl had married and gone away.

McKee put the mug back on a shelf. A brother who had disliked Veronica . . . The seeds of these crimes could lie somewhere in the past—as in what case, when you got right down to it, didn't they? Character versus environment and training about fifty-fifty. As the twig is bent—"How old would Charles be now?"

Hilliard did a little mental arithmetic. "Let's see—somewhere in his middle fifties if he's still alive. But, Inspector," he looked at McKee and shook his head, "if you're figuring along the line your questions seem to indicate, even if Charles did come back here for some reason he'd never lay a finger on Mary Dane. She was always very good to him and he was deeply devoted to her."

"I see." McKee turned his attention to the closet. There were several spots of candle grease on the floor. He thought of Steele's idea late the previous night that there had been someone in the dining room with a light, who had put it out or blown it out when he was on his way to the kitchen for coffee during their vigil with the dying Gomez. At the sound of his advance the light had vanished.

He had felt the presence of somebody near him. The

impression had been strong. Someone armed with a candle searching the closet and pocketing the object in the black box? Quite probably, McKee decided. It got them no closer to the identity of who this person was. It could have been anyone in the hacienda—although they were all supposedly asleep in their separate rooms. Supposedly, that was as far as it went. In any case the implications were grave.

There was no key in the pockets of the coat Mary wore or on her body—and that meant that her killer had removed it.

Someone who was at El Toro during the last thirty-odd hours—and who was still there, cloaked in anonymity—either that or it could have been the man who had lain on the cot in Gomez's room in the barn and who had followed him and Steele back to the house.

The thing in the box was gone but there might be something else here that would be illuminating. McKee started probing shelf after shelf, and paused abruptly. From outside somewhere there was a shout, torn by the thin wail of the wind. It sounded like a shout for help.

The Scotsman left the closet in a hurry and made for the front door fast, with Hilliard, who had also heard the muffled cry at his heels. "No," McKee said, "stay here with the women, and lock this door behind me," and plunged out into the snow and the water.

11

It was Steele who had done the shouting. McKee found him at the door of the chicken house beyond the archway in the rear courtyard. Steele had had a fall and was splashed with wetness and mud from head to foot. Mrs. Tafoya was inside the chicken house, lying on the straw-littered floor near a row of small coops. Above them a parcel of white hens in a huddle on a perch fluttered drowsy wings protestingly at the light, and a white rooster marched up and down belligerently on a rafter in front of them, red comb flaring. The raw dampness in the place was bone-piercing.

"I didn't dare move her, I was afraid to," Steele said, wiping his muddy face with an elbow. "That's why I yelled in the hope of someone hearing." McKee nodded and bent over Mrs. Tafoya. Her hat had fallen off and her slicker was beaded with melted snow. Blood seeped from a small cut near one temple but her pulse was strong and her breathing even. She didn't appear to be badly hurt.

At his touch her eyelids fluttered. She opened her

eyes, stared blankly up at him and closed them again. Thinking what she was going to say—planning it?—McKee speculated cynically. He put her arm down and straightened. "What exactly did happen out here, Steele?" he asked.

Lighting a cigarette with numbed fingers the younger man said, "That's exactly it, Inspector. Nothing. I didn't get to first base or anywhere near it. After you asked me to have a look for her"—he waved at the shapeless huddle with the averted face that was Mrs. Tafoya—"I checked first to see that her car was under the portal. Then I started over in this direction. I had a lantern, sure, but it was about as useful in the snow and the darkness as a match. Just as I got near this place, when I was about twenty feet away, a man ran out slamming the door behind him. He saw me all right, or anyhow he saw the lantern. 'Stand not upon the order of your going'—he took off like a shot out of a cannon. I went after him as fast as I could, I could just barely make him out ahead of me through the snow—and then, when I'd gone only half a dozen yards or so, I fell head over heels over a damn barrel lying out there on its side and by the time I got to my feet and got my wits back there wasn't a smell of my man anywhere, and not a sound either."

"And after that you came in here and found Mrs. Tafoya lying on the floor just as she is now?"

"That's right. I was scared when I looked at her. Her eyes were closed and at first I thought she was dead, then I saw she was breathing."

The rooster was still marching up and down before his now quieter hens. McKee glanced around the interior of the flimsy shed. The man who had fled Gomez's room in the barn after the discovery of Mary Dane's body in the loose box last night could have sought shelter in here . . . There was a pile of straw in a corner that when pulled over him would keep him fairly warm. Granting that he had, Mrs. Tafoya's unexpected appearance would naturally frighten him if he was hiding out deliberately—and it began to seem like it. An attack on her and flight? . . . A moment later McKee was sure of it. A broken egg shell glimmered palely near one of the coops. The shell had been sucked dry. There were four more of them thrown behind another coop. Sustenance, food of a sort, adequate enough if you were hungry.

A search for the fugitive in the falling snow and the now complete darkness would be useless, and in any case the woman on the floor in the cold in wet shoes and stockings ought to be got under cover immediately. If nothing else she had had a nasty shock.

He said to Steele, "We'd better get her inside." They didn't have to carry Mrs. Tafoya. Her consciousness was rapidly returning. When they raised her to her feet she was able to walk, leaning on McKee's arm. He kept close to the house walls, where the water was only seven or eight inches deep. Carrying the lantern Steele led the way across the rear courtyard and under the cottonwood tree to the kitchen door. The door was locked. Jackson opened it at McKee's hail.

Light after darkness, warmth after cold; the logs in the long fireplace burned up brightly and the oil lamp was a comfortable yellow glow. McKee put Mrs. Tafoya in a chair close to the hearth and she sank back, pushing a strand of damp hair from her forehead. The others were there, the girl and Rita Mole and Hilliard, Mrs. Fergusson and Ward. Shocked exclamations at the blood on Mrs. Tafoya's face, questions, "What happened? . . . Good God . . . Where was she?" Hilliard produced a silver flask and McKee poured brandy into a glass Mrs. Fergusson handed him.

"A little water, please," Mrs. Tafoya said in a faint voice. "I'll be all right in a minute." She sipped her drink and after another couple of minutes she told them what had happened.

Her story was as brief and as inconclusive as Steele's. She had gone out to the chicken house with food for the hens, a bucket of scraps, and she was carrying a lantern. When she got near the chicken house the lantern blew out but she managed to find the door and get inside and close the door behind her to keep the snow from blowing in. There were matches in her pocket and she got down on one knee. Before she could even strike a match, light came from another source, a sudden flood of it. She turned her head and found herself looking into the glare of a big flashlight and half blinded by it.

In spite of the warmth of the fire she was shivering. She took another sip of her drink. The man who held the light focused on her was in front of the door, between it and her. He had a gun in his other hand. Before she could scream or make a move he struck out at her and she fell to the floor. She wasn't conscious of anything after that until she came to and found the Inspector there and Mr. Steele and no one else. "I guess I fainted . . . Stupid—but I—I was pretty frightened."

Her watery smile had something pathetic, childlike, about it. "*Scared*—I should think you *would* be," Jill Sheppard exclaimed, bringing her a cup of hot coffee. "What a perfectly *ghastly* experience. It must have been horrible."

"I'll say . . . Poor lady." Jackson rolled his cigar around in his mouth commiseratingly, and shook his head, eyeing her as though he were measuring her for one of his girdles. Mrs. Fergusson as usual said nothing. Her cast-iron imperturbability seemed proof against any shock. Not for the first time McKee reflected that she certainly hadn't been lucky in her choice of a Shangri-La for herself and the husband who was to join her shortly, a choice that still appeared incongruous to him.

Mrs. Mole was also silent, but not stoical. Far from it. Her mouth drooping pathetically, her white eyelids half covering her eyes, she had an air of acute but silent suffering, of "How much more am I going to be able to *bear* in this dreadful place, with these dreadful *people?*"

Hilliard was preoccupied with what to do. "That fellow out there, whoever he is, had a gun. For all we know he may be desperate. We're not safe or won't be while he's at large."

Ward suggested eagerly, "Why don't we go out right now and try to corner him, sir? We ought to be able to do it—there are five of us, five men against one."

Jackson was aghast at this suggestion. He would have none of it. In his earnestness he took his cigar completely out of his mouth. "That's foolish talk, son. Very foolish. Just stop and think a minute. The fellow out there's got a gun and you can be sure it's loaded. Figure it for yourself. We'd have to have lights to get anywhere and he could pick us off one by one before you could say Jack Robinson. How about it, Inspector?"

McKee was forced to agree. With the snow and the darkness the visibility was practically nil and anyone carrying a flashlight or a lantern would be a sitting duck. The thing to do was secure the house for the night and wait until morning came before making a search. Then it could be done competently and with more hope of success. He was convinced that the man hanging around the hacienda wasn't a chance traveler taking refuge from the storm. If so he would have come out of hiding long before this. No, he was there for a definite purpose. It might or might not have anything to do with the Danes and Gomez, it might be one of these others at El Toro he was concerned with. The one person it certainly was not was Mrs. Tafoya. He hadn't hurt her, to speak of. She had surprised him in his hiding place and all he had wanted to do was to get away from her.

McKee left the kitchen and returned to the dining room and his interrupted examination of the closet. After he strangled her, Mary Dane's killer had taken the key of the closet from her body, probably from one of the deep pockets of her heavy windbreaker. He had done this with a purpose in mind. This raised two questions: how had the killer known what particular lock the key fitted? and why, after the killer removed the contents of the black box, hadn't he relocked the door of the closet behind him?

Both questions answered themselves almost immediately. Sending light this way and that in the chilly gloom McKee caught a bright gleam in a crevice in the piñon boards of the flooring. Something had fallen into a crack between the innermost one and the wall. Whatever the object was it was a good four inches down. He had a nail file in his pocket. He took it out and fished patiently. It took five minutes and considerable maneuvering to extract the thing. It was the key to the closet. The key was small and thin. Attached to the haft was a little strip of leather labeled "Dining Room Cupboard."

What must have happened was plain. The killer had evidently dropped it last night in his agitation when Steele had come along, and after Steele had gone on into the kitchen he hadn't dared to linger and try to retrieve the key for fear of being discovered by Steele on his return journey. That must have been it. McKee went on with his scrutiny of the shelves. The only thing of interest he found was a ledger on the top shelf toward the back; he was well over six feet but he had to stretch to reach it.

The ledger was the usual type. It was bound in heavy gray boards, with "Accounts" printed across the front and Veronica Dane's name was written on the flyleaf. He opened it. The first page was dated January first of the current year. He began leafing through it quickly. Veronica had died on the fourth of March. She might have recorded something of moment before she died . . . He skimmed through January and on into February, up until the twentieth—and that was all. There wasn't any more. The pages from the twentieth to the fourth of March inclusive had been torn out by the roots. The rest of the ledger was blank.

12

"So there *was* a light, and I did hear someone in here last night," Steele said. "I think so, in fact I'm sure of it." McKee finished locking the closet door after two horses had been stolen, but there might possibly be fingerprints. He dropped the key in a pocket.

"Yes. You heard someone all right, Steele. You heard Mary Dane's killer—and Gomez's." The Scotsman's face built itself into harsh planes in the light of the candle Steele had brought in from the kitchen with him. The dining room was a cave filled with shadows, the living room beyond a larger cave with snow driving past the dark windows. McKee waved at the closet. "Anyone here in the hacienda could have been in there less than twenty-four hours ago and could have removed those final pages from this ledger of Veronica Dane's."

Steele pushed his hands deeper into his pockets. It was getting colder. The air was icy. He could see his breath coming out in white puffs. In spite of his interest he yawned cavernously.

"God, I'm tired," he said. "I could cork off for a week —and you look as fresh as a daisy."

"Join the police force and learn to go without sleep in ten easy lessons." McKee looked at his watch. It was five minutes after eight. There was a long night ahead and he was going to need Steele later on. It would have taken a number of men to do an adequate job of policing but at least two were better than one. Without too much difficulty he persuaded the younger man to lie down for a couple of hours on one of the sofas in the living room wrapped in a blanket from Ward's bedroom. That done, he returned to the kitchen with the ledger under his arm.

No change. Business as usual. Warmth and lamp and firelight. Gleams of copper here and there on the smoke-stained walls. The closely drawn curtains over the windows shut out the night and the falling snow. No one glanced at McKee with any particular interest as he came in. Rita Mole and Hilliard were playing two-handed bridge at one end of the long table and were absorbed in their cards. At the other end Mrs. Fergusson mended a small hooked rug doggedly and badly. She wasn't much of a sewer. The long needle flashed as she pulled it in and out of the heavy material.

In a bad light, her back to the room as usual, Mrs. Tafoya read steadily through the five-and-ten-cent spectacles, or appeared to be doing so. Jackson dozed in a corner, legs stretched out in front of him, his hands folded across his stomach—and the money belt—a handkerchief over his eyes, and on the far side of the hearth the girl and Ward talked intermittently and gazed into the flames.

McKee took a chair midway along the table and began going through page after unrewarding page of the ledger for a possible gleaning and listened to the girl and Ward with half an ear.

No, Miss Sheppard said, she didn't know this part of the country at all but her sister did. Rita had been out here quite a lot as a young girl visiting school friends. That was when she first met Henry—Mr. Hilliard. Later they had all got to know each other well in New York. "New York"

—Ward had never been there. The blue eyes under his thatch of sandy hair were wistful. He'd sure like to see it, the skyline and the big ships and the river, he had never been out of New Mexico except once to Phoenix and once to Denver with his older brother when he was a kid. Traveling cost a pile of money and he didn't expect he'd ever get a chance to go east.

So Rita Mole was familiar with this part of the country. Interesting, the Scotsman thought, going on methodically with his tiresome task. It might or might not be important. The truth was that until they were free of this place and the statements and backgrounds of all these people were adequately gone into and checked, very little real progress would be made.

Presently Mrs. Fergusson put down her sewing and got up with her usual air of decision. A scratch meal was laid out at the end of the table and she put a fresh pot of coffee on. Ham and pickles and bread and butter and a pot of jam. No one ate much except Jackson, who roused at the sight and smell of food. "Ham and pickles go good," he announced approvingly, his mouth full.

His audience was lethargic. Occasionally someone would go to a window, lift the edge of a curtain, peer out and announce that it was still snowing. They were like a group of strangers at an airport waiting for a plane that was long overdue and might never arrive. But there was more than that in the room. Vacant glances, idle remarks broken off short, a jerky movement on someone's part, a stare at nothing—there was fear there, the feel and smell of it. And why not, with a man outside the walls perhaps prowling around them armed with a gun—on top of all the rest that had happened in this old hacienda in a little over twenty-four hours.

Oh yes, the spurious air of peace was entirely fictitious and might smash at any moment. Watch it. Meanwhile Mc-Kee kept on reading about the ranch business, profit and loss. It was mostly loss; as far as El Toro went its profits were on the skids. A poor price for the hundred acres of woodlot . . . Steers down sharply . . . Sold Betsey's calf. Then two items in succession caught his eye. The first was a cryptic "Sent M. the usual. With things as they are it's getting to be a real drain. One of these days will have to do something about it."

M.—for what? Not her sister. Mary lived in the house with her and it would be unnecessary to send her anything. "The usual" that was getting to be a real drain sounded like money . . . Blackmail? It wasn't very probable. Veronica Dane didn't appear to have been a woman who would submit to being victimized tamely . . . The second item was a note that the Travez had been well stocked earlier and there ought to be plenty of trout when the season came round. Gomez said they needed a new pair of oars.

Oars . . . Oars meant a boat. And a boat meant a way of escape, a means of vanishing into the blue without trace before the police finally arrived. That was if anyone knew where the boat was put up. Possibly the man who had knocked Mrs. Tafoya down in the hen house early that evening had already found it. The Scotsman paused in his task, lit a cigarette, and asked Hilliard about hunting and fishing in these mountains.

The hunting was excellent, Hilliard said, looking up from his cards. "Wildcat and bear and jack rabbit." He added that the fishing was good, too; Travez Creek bordered the Dane land to the north and east.

Jackson put down his coffee cup and rubbed his plump hands enthusiastically and beamed. "Ah, trout, now. You take a rainbow trout from one of these here mountain streams and you couldn't sink a tooth in anything better. No, sir. Believe you me. Wonderful, simply wonderful. Tender as the tenderest chicken—and what a flavor. Oh, boy."

Steele came into the kitchen then. He had had only a

little over an hour's sleep but he looked rested and his eyes were clear. As he walked into the room the girl left her seat beside Ward and got up and went over and perched herself on the arm of Hilliard's chair, her shoulder companionably against his.

If it was intended as a slap at Steele it had no apparent effect on him. He didn't even glance in her direction. He proceeded to make himself a ham sandwich and reached for the mustard. "Here you are, sir." Jackson was sympathetic toward anyone's culinary requirements. Pushing it toward Ward he jostled Mrs. Fergusson's sewing basket and the basket tipped up and fell to the floor, spilling its contents broadcast. Spools of thread rolled in every direction. Ward and Jill Sheppard and Mrs. Tafoya and Jackson retrieved them, the fat man panting and red in the face from the exertion of stooping.

Mrs. Fergusson's darning needle couldn't be found, although they looked everywhere.

She was annoyed. She said she had stuck it into a tuft of wool when she got up to make the coffee. "It *must* be here someplace," she insisted. "It's the only big needle I have . . ."

She picked up the lamp on the center table and played light downward. But the darning needle was nowhere in evidence. Handing her a thimble that had bounced under his feet Hilliard said that it was probably in one of the cracks between the bricks with which the kitchen was floored. Some of them were deep. "It'll show up tomorrow in daylight."

McKee said nothing. It was a small happening, but he didn't like it. It made him uneasy. The needle was long and sharp, a miniature stiletto that would be easy to conceal. Fitted into a handle it would make a swift, silent and efficacious weapon. Have a look for it later on when he was alone.

Shortly after that Rita Mole stifled a yawn and announced that early as it was she was going to bed, and got up. "Coming, Jill?" "I suppose I might as well." Their departure was the signal for a general move. Snow was still falling and the bedrooms were going to be cold. At Hilliard's suggestion empty bottles of various sizes and shapes were brought in from the scullery and filled with hot water from the big kettle on the stove and candles were produced from the diminishing supply. General good nights; before half-past ten the kitchen was empty except for Steele and McKee.

Before he went Ward had obligingly built up a good fire. Jill Sheppard had complimented him on his abilities in that line and he flushed with pleasure and said, "Scout training, I guess, miss." When they were alone watching licking flames circle the fresh logs, Steele listened to the Scotsman's account of what he had found earlier in Mrs. Tafoya's suitcase under her bed.

"Her hair's a dingy mouse color now . . . You think it was—is under that stuff, probably another color, white, or blonde . . . ?" He groped in memory for a more accurate picture of her as she had been when he saw her somewhere before, and shook his head with a frown. A pail, a mop or scrubbing brush, Mrs. Tafoya down on her knees . . . "As I recall her, Inspector, she looked very much as she looks now . . ."

"But it *was* in the East?"

"Yes, certainly, I know that much . . ." Steele's eyes narrowed. "Wait a minute . . . Now I think back it seems to me someone pronounced her name . . ." He sat up and slapped a palm on the arm of his chair. "Got it," he said triumphantly. "What a lame brain—you'd think I'd have remembered it after that envelope you found in Veronica Dane's desk with the return address on it. Her name was Adams, too, the same as the one on the back of the envelope, and I'm pretty sure it was Mrs."

"Even if you can't pin it to a definite place, have you

any idea of how long ago it was that you saw her?" McKee asked, and Steele nodded.

"I've a pretty good idea. It was at least three or four months ago—but that's not what's troubling me. Why should I remember her *at all*? That's the question. There's certainly nothing unusual about her. Cleaning women you come on doing floors in offices or houses don't usually impress themselves on your recollection so strongly, to such an extent. There must be some reason, there's got to be—but I'm damned if I can root it out. She could have married since, of course, but her name was Adams then—that much I'm dead sure of. Does it help any, Inspector?"

Watching a blue flame dancing along a crack in a stick of piñon McKee said, "If this woman is the same Adams, it gives us a third link between the people here now and the Danes."

"A third?"

"Yes. There's Ward, whose mother used to work here years ago, and whom Mary Dane both wrote to and went occasionally to see; then there's Hilliard whose family were both friends and neighbors of the Danes for a long while and who knew them well himself when he was younger— and now there's this Mrs. Tafoya, whose name appears to have been Adams three or four months ago. As you say, she may have married again. If so she must have charms we wot not of . . . They certainly don't show on the surface, also there's no accounting for tastes."

The wind, which had dropped for a while was beginning to rise again. It rushed around the house in long wailing cadences, stirring the curtains at the windows, creeping in along the floor. Listening to it absently Steele was seized like the rest of those stranded travelers with a strong desire to get away from the place, an almost overpowering desire. The purpose for which he had impulsively started west was a washout. He realized that now. He had been barking up the wrong tree. His calculations were erroneous. Jill Sheppard was genuinely in love with Hilliard and they were going to be married and that was that. Even his animosity against Rita Mole had gradually faded, lost its steam. With a woman of her type it was perfectly natural that she should want her sister to marry money with a big M. Let the whole thing go and forget about it. That was the advice he would certainly give to anyone else in the same boat.

The ticking of the clock was loud against the inner stillness. His eyelids were heavy again. The fire burned up, clear and bright. Suddenly there was a noise in the chimney and a puff of smoke billowed out into the room.

McKee glanced at it and his glance sharpened. He got to his feet. Crossing to the entry he unlocked the outside door and opened it a slit, a hand on his police positive. With the other hand he switched on his flashlight. Outside in the long beam of light there was snow and darkness and nothing else. But now the snow was coming from the other direction. The wind had changed abruptly, shifting from the east into the northwest. He turned light downward. He couldn't be sure but it seemed to him that already the water blowing sideways in ripples was appreciably lower and beginning to recede.

Closing and locking the door he returned to the fire. More smoke. Steele had moved his chair back and sideways from the hearth. He was coughing. McKee said, "I think the storm will soon be over, for the moment anyhow, the worst of it. By morning the valley ought to be pretty well drained off and fairly clear of water, and the creek back in its banks."

"That means we can all get away from this place, as soon as our cars dry out. I don't think there's very much wrong with mine, I simply skidded into the ditch."

Steele sounded weary. His voice was flat. McKee said, "No, you can't—you can't leave here, no one can, until the police manage to get here. They'll want statements from every one of you personally."

The night wore slowly on. At 3:00 A.M. the Scotsman took a swing through the darkened hacienda. There was no one stirring. Sonorous snores came from behind Jackson's door; for the rest, nothing but silence except for the fading whisper of the wind beyond the stout walls. Another trip at around five, more darkness and silence on the second floor except that this time Jackson wasn't snoring. He started down the stairs. He was at the foot of them when above his head a door closed softly.

Switching off his light he retraced his steps. At the top he switched light on again. Mrs. Fergusson in a dark blue wool bathrobe was advancing toward him from the right. Her room was to the left at the other end of the corridor.

She surveyed him composedly. "Oh," she said, "it's you, Inspector. I thought I heard someone, and that I'd better get up and see what was going on."

She still wore her earrings. There were stockings on her feet under the slippers. She didn't look like a woman who had been roused by a noise and had got up hastily to investigate. As if she felt his skepticism she went on more vehemently. "I couldn't seem to get to sleep although I usually don't have any trouble. I never thought I'd hate a place so much . . . I can't imagine now what made me take it. All I know is that, option or no option, I'm finished with it and I'm getting out as soon as I can."

McKee nodded his understanding. "I can't say I blame you, Mrs. Fergusson."

She gave him a keen glance, veiled it instantly, said good night, walked off to her own room and closed the door.

The Scotsman was halfway down the stairs for the second time when he heard another sound from below. It came from beyond the dining room. It was small and faint but unmistakable. It was the phone ringing. He took the rest of the stairs in a flying leap, hit the living-room floor, skidded upright, and raced for the pantry.

13

When he picked up the phone it was live and he could hear voices distantly. They were tangled at first, then he sorted them out. A telephone repair man named Pete was talking to another one named Joe. A string of numbers. "I'm at pole 426, are you getting me clear, Pete?" "Sure am, nice and clear, amigo . . ." A woman cut in excitedly, "Operator, operator." "Get off the line, lady—we're testing," one of the men said and was interrupted by an excited flood of Spanish from someone else. Then the wire abruptly went dead.

McKee tried it again half a dozen times during the next twenty minutes without result. There was no dial tone. In the end it was the state police who called him. Speaker had managed to get through to them. An officer, who announced himself as Lieutenant Menendez, said the rancher had arrived at the barracks on horseback at around 3:00 A.M. But the lines were still down and there was no way of reaching El Toro until now.

McKee gave the lieutenant at the other end of the wire a succinct account of what had happened at the Dane ranch and a list of names to check on. They talked tersely for three or four minutes. Then the lieutenant said that they'd do what they could as fast as they could and meanwhile they'd keep in touch.

McKee thanked him, replaced the instrument in its cradle and thought for a moment. With the wires in the condition in which they were, it would be extremely difficult if not impossible to get through to New York. He lifted the receiver again and called James Ringrose.

As soon as he was connected and announced himself, a volley of hearty curses filled with relief poured into his ear. "My God, McKee, I didn't know what had happened to you, thought you might be over a cliff somewhere. You should have followed the directions I gave you more carefully, old man . . ."

He pricked up his ears at the mention of El Toro. "What's that, what's that? The Dane ranch, eh? Sure I know the Danes, or did. Ran into the old girl at the state fair two years ago, she copped first prize at the rodeo—great rider. Used to know the younger brother, too—what was his name? Charles, that's right. Came up here to hunt a couple of seasons. Brought his daughter with him, pretty little thing she was—Laura, Lily—I forget. It was back in the late nineteen thirties."

"Charles?" As far as Ringrose knew, Charles was abroad somewhere—Portugal, he thought, his wife was Portuguese. Handsome woman. She and Veronica didn't quite hit it off, but then sisters-in-law. Quite a character Veronica Dane was. Bit of a museum piece, but impressive, very impressive. When would McKee be along?

The Scotsman said he wouldn't and explained. The colonel was horrified. The younger sister killed! And a man about the place, too? Good God almighty. What was the world coming to? "Terrible age we live in." After some more talk he agreed to call New York with the message that the Inspector would be detained for possibly another forty-eight hours and McKee rang off.

The house still apparently slumbered. In spite of the ringing of the phone no one seemed to have roused. Ward slept on in his room, or at least his door remained closed, and Steele continued to doze in his chair before the kitchen fire. McKee went to the windows above the sink and pulled the curtains back.

The night was over at last. Dawn was just beginning to break in the east, no more than a grayness as yet above towering peaks, their tops obscured by clouds. But the snow had definitely stopped.

McKee went to the back door to inspect the water level in the courtyard. A cold dawn freshness; the darkness lingered down here in the valley. Objects were only just visible. Where, he wondered, was the man who had sheltered first in the barn and then in the chicken house? Well, there were plenty of other places to hide, in one or another of the outbuildings, for instance.

The water had all but seeped away. There wasn't more than four or five inches of it left under the drive of the breeze that was sweeping it lower down the valley at a lively pace. In another hour or two it would be gone. Flotsam and jetsam showing up everywhere; his eye lit on a floating stick moving briskly toward the house just beyond the trunk of the cottonwood tree. It drifted past, within twenty feet of where McKee stood. He stared at it. No, there wasn't any doubt. The gray stick was an oar with a broken blade. An oar—an oar meant a boat as he had figured last night . . .

The Scotsman closed and locked the door. The lieutenant at the state barracks had said that it might be some time before they could get men up to El Toro. A few of the roads were open but the majority were still impassable with washouts, and bridges and trees down. McKee knew that his own job for the moment was to keep the cast of characters on stage and safe in the hacienda until he was relieved by the local authorities. He began making rounds past the still somnolent Steele on into the living room and up the stairs.

He didn't have far to look. The bedroom doors could only be secured on the inside by a nib that held the latch in place. Hilliard's, Mrs. Fergusson's, Jill Sheppard's, and Rita Mole's were solid in the frames. Not so Jackson's and Mrs. Tafoya's. Their rooms were empty—and Mrs. Tafoya's suitcase was gone from under her bed. So were the few clothes that had hung in her wardrobe. He made for the back stairs and the kitchen fast. He couldn't leave here. Steele, he thought, Steele was the only one who could take off.

Less than fifteen minutes later Steele was putting the hacienda behind him under the wheels of Mrs. Fergusson's new car. He wasn't sorry to leave the accursed place and he had agreed at once when the Inspector told him what he wanted him to do. It was necessary to drive with extreme care. The mud was, or at any rate seemed to be, practically bottomless. He sat upright peering through the windshield. The receding water had left a varied lot of debris in its wake; a rusty ten-gallon can and assorted pieces of wood large and small loomed up in the early light.

According to the Inspector, either together or separately Mrs. Tafoya and Jackson had flown the coop, leaving the hacienda at some unknown hour through the door at the end of the transverse corridor by the simple expedient of pushing the bolt back. It had a snap lock on it and could be opened from inside but not from outside.

Standing under the portal in the rear courtyard McKee had done something to the engine under the hood of Mrs. Fergusson's long pale green sedan to start the keyless ignition, remarking virtuously that it was a citizen's duty to help the police if called upon and able to do so and she was sure to agree when he explained that to her. Whether there was or wasn't a boat, Mrs. Tafoya's car was gone from its place, which was all they could tell about her movements for certain. Steele had readily agreed to try and get a line on her and on Jackson—that was if he could. They had a head start, sure, but beyond that they would be subject to the same road conditions as he would, and the same hazards.

Breathing the fresh air, he pulled it deep into his lungs with a sensation of freedom. Yes, he was glad to get out of the hacienda with its smell of age and decay, gladder still to get away from Hilliard and Jill Sheppard. Enough was enough. Neither of the fugitives was anywhere in sight on the grounds that were visible on either hand. The bridge across the creek was still intact but it was awash with at least a foot of water. Halfway down the driveway he had to detour around Jackson's stranded car, one of the doors wide open where he had dived out into last night's flood. Then the gate with El Toro over it, and the public road. He got out there to study the surface.

Unmistakably, the tracks were clear in the mud; Mrs. Tafoya's Chevy had turned right in the direction of Albuquerque. Mountains reared up darkly to right and left. They were mostly veiled in cloud. The descent out of them was steep and the surface, on adobe mud, sticky going. Then, after two or three miles, he struck hardtop, and after that it was easier.

His wrist watch said five minutes of seven when he topped a small rise and saw the city of Albuquerque itself spread out in the broad valley below, a vast heterogeneous mass of low roofs broken by tree masses and running clear to a line of mesas or perhaps extinct volcanos far to the west.

In the now rain-washed air—the place was well over a mile high—distances were almost impossible to measure. What looked to be a couple of miles away might turn out to be twenty or forty or fifty. Nowhere as far as he could see on the serpentine downward track was another vehicle moving. Then rounding a curve a little farther on he caught sight of two, perhaps a thousand feet lower down.

The first vehicle was a school bus, painted bright yellow. It was too early for school yet, and it was probably empty. A short distance behind it and making good time was Mrs. Tafoya's old Chevy—or at any rate it looked remarkably like hers. Try and get closer to it and make sure.

Steele put on a burst of speed, and instantly regretted it. Even the hard surface was tacky with damp mud and he went into a half-spin on the lip of a gorge. By the time he had righted the car, to his disappointment the Chevy had vanished. Watch for crossroads from that point on . . . Three more miles of twists and turns without break. There were no crossroads and no side lanes either so the Chevy had to be somewhere out ahead. He was getting well down now. It was a fold in the foothills that had obscured his view.

Behind him the sun was coming up over the wall of the mountains to the east. It touched the far-away mesas with a long line of light. Then he descended a slight grade. The mesas disappeared. Almost on the level. The immense valley stretching out in front of him appeared to be as flat as a pancake. Just before he hit bottom he caught a single glimpse of the Chevy on the straggling outpost of the city proper about a quarter of a mile ahead. Then he finally hit bottom. Small flat-roofed adobe houses began to appear. Horses and sheep and cattle grazed in the fields.

In the valley, if there had been snow, it had vanished but there was plenty of water around. Here and there some oddly shaped trees were turning faintly green at their tops. Traffic sprang up magically. Cars and trucks were turning into the main road west from muddy lanes and out of driveways in increasing numbers. Steele kept his foot down on the accelerator. He didn't want to lose the Chevy, neither did he want to get too close to it.

The Inspector thought it possible Jackson might have fled the hacienda by boat but there was no proof of it, he might just as well have gone with Mrs. Tafoya. Why had they both found it imperative to get away from El Toro? Were they connected in some way? Was there a concealed link between them in spite of their appearing to be strangers to each other? And had either or both overheard the telephone call from the state police, and was that what had impelled them to headlong flight?

One of these questions was answered less than twenty minutes later. Jackson was not in the car with Mrs. Tafoya. She was alone behind the wheel. The long level road they were both on ended in a stop sign at another main road running north and south. The Chevy turned north into this road and with the sun well above the mountains now, he caught a clear glimpse of the woman as she signaled and swung right into what a sign said was Fourth Street at around the center of the city. It wasn't too crowded yet but the sidewalks and the streets were starting to fill up. It was flanked with garages and shops and a supermarket, second-hand stores, service stations, and banks—all the buildings were squat and ugly and unimpressive.

After a mile or so of this beyond a railroad crossing they were pretty well clear of the business section. Houses now, with empty fields between, most of them with horses in them. An occasional chili parlor or group of small shops. A couple of motels, and signs advertising Worms and Ice. Fishermen in this aridity? It seemed incredible . . . Where the devil, Steele wondered, was the woman ahead of him going? Fourth Street was Route 85 and led north to Santa Fe. Was that where she was bound for? It was not.

At Ranchitos, a road running west toward the mesas, she turned again. Real country now; plowed fields and more and more horses, chickens and a cow with her calf. Immense cottonwoods were interspersed with poplars and Chinese elms. The bright gleam of forsythia and daffodils in gardens. Another turn, this time into a small side road named Guadalupe Trail.

Following the Chevy along this, Steele dropped back. The speed posted was twenty-five miles an hour. Mrs. Tafoya was also proceeding more slowly.

Houses were set well back in spacious grounds for the most part. Then a poorish section of square boxes made of old adobe brick, eroded and crumbling away in places. In spite of the rain in isolated pools the yards were already dusty, with a few chickens, and weird wooden shacks at the back built out of whatever rubble came to hand. It was into the last one of these that Mrs. Tafoya had turned the Chevy. Rounding a bend Steele almost ran past without seeing it. The car stood some twenty-five feet in from the road. It was empty. Mrs. Tafoya was evidently inside the miserable house.

Steele drove on some fifty feet around another turn and pulled up as far off the narrow trail as it was possible to get. McKee's instructions to him had been to find out if he could where Mrs. Tafoya and Jackson went to earth and then get in touch with the police. He hadn't found Jackson but he had found her. It was easy to say notify the police but he was in a quandary. If he left here to go in search of the main road and a telephone—there were boxes along it at intervals—the woman might take off again while he was gone. No, that wouldn't answer. He got out to do a little reconnoitering.

The cover was thin. There were open-fenced fields on both sides of the lane almost up to the house into which Mrs. Tafoya had vanished. No bushes or convenient shrubs. Then he came on the ditch, and recognized it for what it was from what he had read. It was one of the countless irrigation ditches that kept the north valley green and fertile in the surrounding deserts. There was no water in the ditch now and it was fairly deep, perhaps five feet. It ran parallel with the driveway on which the Chevy stood. Steele dropped down into it and moved carefully through dead leaves and an assortment of rusty cans at the bottom, crouched almost double. He went on for ten yards or so, until he was level with Mrs. Tafoya's parked car. Then he raised his head.

The view was not an inspiring one. A backyard without so much as a blade of grass in it and an outhouse near the fence at the rear; the place evidently boasted no modern conveniences. A cream-colored horse with a black mane and tail was tied to a rickety post, and the ubiquitous chickens pecked industriously at a handful of weeds near a broken child's swing made of an old tire. Except for the animals nothing moved in this abomination of desolation. And the silence was deep. What to do?

McKee's directions had been clear. Not to attempt action himself but if he ran Mrs. Tafoya to earth to leave the rest entirely to the police. For some reason or other he was oddly reluctant to do that. In spite of her unprepossessing appearance and bumbling manner, there had been something about the woman he liked, although he couldn't put his finger on what it was. No, not the police—yet anyhow, he decided; wait a bit first and see what gave here. He was in no hurry to get back to the hacienda up there in the Sandias, the sullen blue giants faintly visible far to the east.

A dog barked somewhere, then on the far side of the Chevy and just beyond it a window was thrown up. "One more rinse and we dry," a woman said, and a voice that was Mrs. Tafoya's, and yet oddly not hers, answered. "I don't care much, Bella, just so we get the worst of it out. I'll have it taken care of properly when I get home. I'm late as it is and I've got to hurry."

The sound of water being poured from a jug or pitcher into a basin. The pourer whose name appeared to be Bella said soothingly, "Just a little cupful more, *favorita*. There— now we use the towel."

Home, Steele thought, as soon as I get home, Mrs. Tafoya had said in that subtly different voice. She didn't live here and as she said she did seem to be in a hurry. He fin-

gered a cigarette he didn't light although he wanted a smoke
badly. Mrs. Fergusson's long green sedan was parked around
a bend some hundred yards away. The Inspector had
stressed that it would be better all around if Mrs. Tafoya
didn't know she was being followed. If she went past the
car when she took her departure she would scarcely recognize it as Mrs. Fergusson's, there were thousands of them
on the road. That didn't worry him. What did was that if
she left here shortly and headed north again, back the way
she had come, by the time he got to the sedan and got it
turned around he would have lost her irretrievably.

No voices from inside now. A door had closed. The
two women had probably gone into another room. He flexed
stiff muscles and started back along the ditch to the road.
He was at the far end of it, and almost at the road itself,
when Mrs. Tafoya and another woman, a stout black-eyed
woman in a housedress came out of the front door of the
square adobe box.

Steele crouched motionless, staring in amazement.
Standing in full sunlight Mrs. Tafoya was pulling on a pair
of gloves. But she wasn't the Mrs. Tafoya of El Toro, bore
no slightest resemblance to her. Watching her through a
screen of small branches where he crouched out of sight,
his jaw dropped. He couldn't see her face, he didn't need
to. Her carriage was enough. The hair that had been a
mousy brown was a deep gold under the brim of a smart
hat, and head high she was poised and erect in a well-cut
coat and skirt, and carried an expensive fur coat flung carelessly over one arm.

He was still gazing after her with a stunned feeling
when she and her companion went around the corner of the
house to the far side. A distant murmur of voices, the slam
of a car door, the soft purr of a motor, then a Lincoln Con-
tinental, long and low and black with a white top, came
down the short driveway with the metamorphosed Mrs.
Tafoya at the wheel and, as he had feared, it swung north,

the way the ancient Chevy had come, and disappeared from view.

Steele's only satisfaction was that as the Lincoln turned he got the license number. It was a New Mexican plate. Under the LAND OF ENCHANTMENT, at which Steele snorted inwardly, was a 1-275.

Less than three minutes later he was back in Mrs. Fergusson's sedan and giving chase to the Lincoln. His luck was out. Before he had gone more than two hundred feet a cumbersome plow turned in ahead of him. The road was too narrow to pass, chafe at the bit as he would, and the plow showed no sign of moving over in response to his horn. When he reached the end of the Guadalupe Trail at long last and glanced up and down Ranchitos there wasn't a single car in sight and he could see for better than a quarter of a mile each way. The Lincoln was fast and a good ten minutes had elapsed. Further pursuit was hopeless. But he might still pull something out of the fire.

Back at the poor rundown house on Guadalupe Trail Mrs. Tafoya had left, he rapped on the door, there was no bell. The stout comfortable woman in the housedress opened to him. She stared stolidly into his face from behind broken wire in what had once been a homemade screen door and shook her head.

"I don't want to buy nothing, nothing at all."

Steele smiled, "Oh, I'm not selling anything," he said agreeably, "and I'm sorry to bother you. But Mrs. Tafoya—"

The woman interrupted him. She nodded vigorously. "*Si, si*—that's my name, yes. What is it you desire, you want?" Her dark stare had grown wary and suspicious.

He said, "You're Mrs. Tafoya?—then I guess it must be another Mrs. Tafoya I'm looking for . . ."

"There was no other Mrs. Tafoyas on this road."

She spoke sharply but Steele was no longer looking at her. His gaze was fastened on a photograph in a silver frame on the mantel shelf above the adobe fireplace behind her to the left. Staring at the photograph hard memory came back in a flash with a sudden revealing rush.

The next instant his view was abruptly cut off. The door was shut in his face and a bolt shot home. Steele didn't linger. He had no desire to. Far from it. Five minutes later he was back in the sedan and on his way to find the nearest telephone and ring El Toro.

14

"Cinderella," McKee said at the other end of the wire, as though he thought Steele had gone slightly mad. *"Cinderella?"*

Steele laughed. "That's right, Inspector. You recall I was puzzled because I told you I didn't see why I *should* remember Mrs. Tafoya down on her knees with a pail and a mop? That was because it was only a half-memory." Steele paused to light a much-needed cigarette. McKee was impatient. "When and where did you meet her and who is she really?"

Steele exhaled a satisfying lungful of smoke. "I met her at a country club in Westchester about four or five months ago—when my sister dragged me there to an entertainment for some charity or other, and Mrs. Tafoya, who called herself that up there at El Toro anyhow, played the part of Cinderella in a short skit. And very good she was . . . Later on in the evening I was introduced to her. She was then, and is now from the glimpse I got of her a little while ago, a beautiful woman and judging from her dress and the jewels she wore at the club that night she seemed to have plenty of money. Also her name was certainly not Tafoya then, it was Adams, Mrs. Adams, as I told you, and she had a daughter with her, a pretty girl of fourteen or so."

He went on methodically with the rest of it, including the number of the car she was driving when she took off after a change of clothes and having her hair washed in the shack on the Guadalupe Trail by the woman whose name *was* Tafoya.

"Probably an old servant, and Mrs. Adams used both her name and her car . . ." McKee said musingly, listening with satisfaction to the inward click, click, click of facts dropping into the proper slots in his mind. Veronica Dane had had a niece on the stage, and Mrs. Adams had been an actress before her marriage, which must have taken place at least fifteen years ago, from the daughter's age. In all probability—in fact there was scarcely a doubt of it—Mrs. Adams was Veronica and Mary Dane's niece. That was why she had been so shaken when Gomez, whom she knew well—she had been brought up at El Toro—was carried into the house that first night . . .

As to why she had returned to the hacienda in what amounted to a disguise and using a false name, that was another question entirely. She must have had a fairly strong reason . . .

He told Steele to hang on and left the phone. A detachment of state police had arrived at the hacienda some time ago and the Scotsman went in search of Officer Petrelli, who was superintending the removal of the two bodies, Gomez's and Mary Dane's, in a local ambulance. Petrelli's car had a two-way radio. Less than five minutes later the report came back.

The 1 on the license plate on the Lincoln meant that the plate had been issued in Santa Fe. The owner was a Mrs. Robert Adams, who had a home in the capital. According to the Santa Fe people the Adamses were highly thought of there. Mrs. Adams' husband had died some years earlier leaving her very well off and she and her daughter, the only child of the marriage, lived in a large house in spacious grounds on La Joya Road. The trooper gave the Inspector the telephone number.

McKee looked at his watch. Mrs. Adams, nee Dane, couldn't be home yet. It was sixty-two odd miles from Albuquerque up to Santa Fe. Call her later, he decided—or better still simply have the state police bring her back for the inquest on both Gomez and Mary Dane that was to be held in the mortuary in the local hospital early the following morning. If necessary a subpoena would have to be issued to her but it probably wouldn't come to that. She was evidently a clever woman. He returned to the phone and gave Steele a quick fill-in.

Hilliard had wanted to get east to his father's ranch but the police said the roads over the crest were impassable so he and the two women, Mrs. Mole and Miss Sheppard, had gone to the nearest inn where they were going to spend the night in order to be present at the autopsy hearing which was set for early next morning. Young Ward was a bit of a mechanic and had dried out the Rolls and they had taken him with them when they went.

"Jackson?" Steele asked and McKee said there was no word of him so far, and no sign either of the man who had fled the chicken house the night before. Mrs. Fergusson had been coldly furious at the appropriation of her car and had demanded and was getting transportation to the same hotel Hilliard and Mrs. Mole and her sister were bound for.

"I told her you'd deliver her car to her there, Steele. I'm leaving here soon and I can pick you up there. In the meantime, if she shows, you might try and keep an eye on her."

Steele hadn't much of a yen for the role of amateur detective but since he had to appear at the inquest and couldn't shake the dust of New Mexico from his feet until it was over, he said resignedly O.K. and rang off.

It was then twenty minutes of ten. Driving back through Albuquerque it seemed to him he had passed with a leap over a gap of several centuries into the middle of this big busy typical Southwest city, but wisps of the nightmare the hacienda had been still clung about him. He badly wanted a shower and fresh clothing, the best he could do was buy a shirt in a haberdashery on Central Avenue and visit a barber shop. After that he drove on to the Del Rio Grande, the hotel Mrs. Fergusson was headed for five or six miles to the northeast. It was a great rambling place that belonged to a bygone era. Before the advent of the automobile it had boasted a sulphur spring no longer in use, and had once been fashionable in the horse and carriage age. Now it was a vast, almost empty shell. The settlement surrounding it was small.

Mrs. Fergusson hadn't arrived at the hotel yet, and Steele left a note for her with the solitary clerk at the ponderous desk saying she would find her car in the parking lot across the street. Then he went into a dim coffee room and ordered bacon and eggs and toast and coffee. He was just finishing when through the archway he saw Rita Mole and Hilliard and Jill Sheppard in the middle of the lobby.

The sight of them infuriated him. His one desire was to put plenty of distance between himself and the three of them. To his relief they didn't enter the coffee room but went at once in the opposite direction preceded by a boy in buttons at a brisk trot carrying what looked to be fifteen pieces of assorted luggage. When they were gone Steele sought a chair in a secluded corner of the lounge and settled down moodily to wait for the arrival of Mrs. Fergusson.

Meanwhile at the hacienda El Toro up in the Sandias the police had finished their work and taken off. The fingerprint men were the last to go. McKee had supplied them with an assortment of prints on various cups and glasses, all properly labeled. They promised they'd get in touch as soon as possible with anything that turned up.

When they began to work he had asked them to pay particular attention to all prints in the late Veronica Dane's bedroom and to Gomez's room in the barn where the odd-man-out had taken shelter before moving on to the chicken house, from which the pseudo Mrs. Tafoya had driven him to a further hiding hole. It certainly wasn't anywhere around at the front of the hacienda, the terrain there was clear and offered no cover whatever. The back was something else again.

Yes, that was the place to keep an eye on. There was a good chance that when he thought the coast was clear of police and the other guests gone, the lurker might consider it safe to emerge from cover. Mrs. Fergusson's unobtrusive exit from the house had been through the front door in the last official car to leave. By twelve noon only McKee and a single trooper remained.

They couldn't be seen from outside by an observer. The trooper patrolled one end of the hacienda, the Inspector the other, both of them standing well back from the windows and making no noise. They didn't even smoke. Half an hour after they took up their vigil, it got results. A soft call from the trooper, Bernie Chavez. McKee joined him in the room that Ward had occupied.

Chavez was pointing toward bales of hay piled in blocks beyond the pump house. Sitting on top of the pile was a man's head with a hat on it, a stained and battered gray felt hat. Just that, nothing more.

The hatted head was a somewhat startling sight. It hadn't been there a second earlier. It swung slowly right and left, then a neck added itself to the head cautiously and after that first one shoulder and then the other wriggled out from an interstice between two bales of hay and the man himself clambered from his hiding place and dropped to the ground.

It was an ingenious hideout, warm, sheltered and with an excellent view. As McKee and the trooper watched intently from deep shadow, the gentleman in the gray hat approached the house. As he disappeared beyond the cottonwood the trooper went silently through the window of the little room and McKee proceeded on into the kitchen. A moment after he got there a sharp rap on the locked back door was followed by a voice.

"It's no use, Etta," the man outside called. "I know you're in there and that the police are gone. You might as well open up, my dear, or I'll be obliged to break a window. Hear me? You can't get away now I've found you. So don't try. It might make me mad."

By that time McKee was in the entryway. Without a word he turned the key in the lock, and slid the bolt back. The man who catapulted himself through the suddenly opened door was small, slight, and under other circumstances would have been dapper. He had the look of it. He was somewhere in his fifties with guileless blue eyes under a brush of silvery hair.

He stared at McKee hard. "Oh . . . Sorry, sir," he said. "I'm looking for—Mrs. Fergusson, who rented this ranch from people named Dane I believe, a week or two ago or thereabouts. Can you tell me where Mrs. Fergusson is?"

McKee wanted to give the trooper plenty of time to get across the courtyard and cut off the fellow's retreat. "She a friend of yours?" he asked pleasantly.

The man in the battered felt hat smiled. "Sometimes and sometimes not. You know how it is . . . She's my wife."

"Oh," McKee said, "I see, yes." There was something vaguely familiar about the man's face . . . He couldn't place it at once. But the trooper did, unhesitatingly. Hurrying up from behind he came level, and stared down at the so-called Mr. Fergusson, his mouth a little open. Then he gave tongue.

"Willie," he all but yelled. "Willie Stokes, or I'm a Dutchman."

The man in the gray hat showed no sign of confusion. He surveyed the trooper calmly from head to foot. "I'm afraid I don't know you, young man, and therefore I am unable to say anything about your—eh—probable ancestry. No."

He shook his head and began brushing wisps of straw from his tweed topcoat. The trooper turned excitedly to McKee. But the Scotsman already knew. Willie Stokes was a confidence man whose record every police department up and down the United States was well acquainted with, he was one of the best in the business. For years he had raked in large sums of money by fraud and had successfully defied the law, but finally, some three years or so earlier, he had been caught on a comparatively petty swindle in Florida and put in the cooler there for a five-year stretch. His time had evidently been cut for good behavior.

The trooper whipped a pair of cuffs out of his pocket. "Hold out your hands, mister."

Stokes made no objection. He said with a twinkle in his eyes, examining McKee's height and the trooper's brawn, "You pay me a compliment, my boy, I'm not as strong as all that—but as you will." He was resigned, philosophical, both then and in the police car that presently arrived in response to the trooper's call, and after that in the state barracks with Lieutenant Menendez.

He was frank, up to a point at any rate. But the Scotsman noted that he made positive statements only on what he knew could be verified. He said that after he was released in Miami for good behavior—"I always try to be coöperative"—he returned to New York, to find his wife had flown the coop, and not empty-handed. He shook his head sadly. He discovered that when she went she had taken with her the contents of a safe deposit box that unfortunately was in both their names. "I know, I know, never trust a woman—but it's a failing of mine." Johnson (in whom McKee recognized Jackson) was her new sweetie pie.

Stokes wasn't particularly interested in either of them, what he did want was his money back. "The savings of a lifetime." He coughed virtuously and refused to name an exact sum. He said he had tracked his wife and Johnson out here through friends.

After he had been charged, removed to a cell and permitted to send for a lawyer, Lieutenant Menendez said to McKee, "He's wanted in Albuquerque for a real estate swindle which netted him eighty or ninety thousand dollars but he'll be out on bail in a couple of hours or I miss my guess. Going to do his own hunting, I think, when he's loose. It's up to us to look slippy."

To the Scotsman's disappointment Stokes was unable, or unwilling, to shed any light on the killing of Mary Dane or the attack on Gomez. In his statement he said that according to his calculations he had arrived at El Toro some twenty minutes or so after McKee and Steele got there. He had hired a car at the Sunlight Garage in Albuquerque to deliver him at the El Toro gates. Contacted, the garage corroborated the call but nothing else, the driver was unavailable, he was stormbound on another run up into the Sandias.

Willie Stokes was evidently the man Mrs. Mole had seen through the drawing-room window at El Toro that first night. As far as the Scotsman went he couldn't be dismissed as inconsequential; he had been in New Mexico before and might have had some connection with the Danes. He and the lieutenant were discussing the case when Bill Speaker called. He talked to both Menendez and McKee. He was shocked and horrified at the news of Mary's death and as soon as he heard it he had rung the Danes' lawyer, Santander, and Santander had volunteered a piece of information that he figured might be useful. He proceeded to give it.

On the morning she left El Toro after turning it over to Mrs. Fergusson, Mary had phoned Santander to say that she would be in his office in a day or two with an envelope apparently containing documents she had found when she was clearing out Veronica's bedroom. The envelope was sealed and across the front of it was written: "To be delivered to Tony Santander in the event of my sudden death."

So that, McKee reflected, was what Mary had left behind her when she went and had returned to get. It was the sealed envelope that had been removed from the ebony box in the dining-room cupboard after she had been killed.

Santander was not in his office when McKee tried to get him, and the lieutenant left word with his secretary to have the lawyer call the barracks as soon as possible. Then the report from the fingerprint bureau came through, in triplicate. Perusing the copy the lieutenant handed him, McKee whistled softly, and Menendez looked up. "Something, Inspector?"

McKee nodded and told him. More pieces falling into place, as he had expected or rather hoped, once contact with the outside world was reëstablished. On the night Gomez died two people had searched Veronica Dane's room where the stricken man lay, probably for the documents Mary Dane had already transferred to the dining-room cupboard. They were the so-called Mrs. Tafoya, whose real name was Adams, nee Dane, and Henry Hilliard. The first searcher was Mrs. Tafoya, her prints were overlaid a number of times by Hilliard's—therefore it was Henry Hilliard who had knocked young Ward out.

Lieutenant Menendez looked both surprised and uncomfortable at this development. The Hilliards were big people in that part of the state. Not only were they well thought of generally but they had friends in high places— and Henry Hilliard was the old man's white-haired boy. Money and influence—Hilliard had been mentioned as a candidate for state senator when the present incumbent's term ran out—to be up against, have to buck.

McKee also looked grave but for a different reason. Hilliard had covered his tracks well, he had been seemingly frank and open throughout, now he had been proved a liar. The man was unaware of this yet. The only one who could implicate him in any way was young Ward, if Ward should chance to remember who had struck him—and Ward was with the Hilliard party in the local hotel. Better get over there and have a talk with Hilliard. Five minutes later he was on his way.

15

"Yes, Inspector." Henry Hilliard fingered the knot of his tie and looked directly at McKee. His stance was easy, his gaze cool and unflurried. "You're quite right. I did go into Veronica Dane's bedroom at El Toro that first night, the night we arrived there, after you and Speaker left the hacienda together." He took a turn up and down the small writing room. He showed no slightest sign of discomposure and his words were measured.

"And coming up on him from behind through the partially open door you struck young Ward over the back of the head and knocked him out cold."

Hilliard winced a little at that but he didn't try to get away from it. He nodded. "I'm afraid I did. I didn't like doing it, certainly. I hated it, but I didn't hurt him badly—and I mean to make it up to him."

"And after he was out you proceeded to search the bedroom thoroughly?"

Another inclination of the well-brushed head. McKee studied him curiously. His regret seemed genuine but by no means overpowering. Faced by a disagreeable necessity he had simply done what he had to do, was what he was saying in effect. A cool customer.

"What were you looking for, Mr. Hilliard? The papers Mary Dane had already transferred to the ebony box in the dining-room cupboard—the locked door of which her killer later opened with a key he took from her body?"

Hilliard stared. His expression was uncomprehending. "I don't believe I quite know what you're talking about, Inspector . . . What I was searching Veronica's room for was something that belonged to me. That's all I can tell you, all I'm at liberty to tell you. If I were the only one involved it would be different perhaps, but I'm not. There are"—he paused for a second and went on—"there are others concerned."

"Mrs. Tafoya?" McKee suggested mildly.

Hilliard was astonished, and slightly amused at this offering. "Mrs.—good God, man, no. Nobody there at the hacienda . . ."

It was at that point that the door of the small room off the lobby opened. It was Mrs. Adams who opened it. She saw them and paused just over the threshold. McKee had expected a considerable change in her appearance but even he was surprised at how much of a change it would be. She was another woman completely and an extremely attractive one at that. It was only by looking very closely indeed that you could see certain points of resemblance, in the eyes mainly, and the breadth of the forehead and the straight delicate nose. Perhaps it was in her carriage and her bearing that the greatest change lay.

She looked composedly from one man to the other. "Am I interrupting a conference? I'm sorry. I didn't know the room was in use." She started to turn away.

McKee said, "Don't go, Mrs. Adams. There are some questions I'd like to ask you—that is, of course, if you're willing to answer them."

"Questions?" Facing him, her brown brows lifted.

"Ask the questions and we'll see, Inspector," she said smiling at him.

She had the same assurance, the same poise as Hilliard. Their faces revealed nothing and they were both clever people. Let your conversation be aye, aye or nay, nay. Don't get flustered, keep calm, admit only what you have to and volunteer nothing.

Mrs. Adams admitted readily that she had searched Veronica's room on the evening of her arrival while Steele slept. "She was my aunt, you know." Her purpose was the same as Hilliard's. She had gone there to get something that belonged to her. "Vero—she hated to be called aunt, didn't like to be reminded of age in any way . . ." She smiled reminiscently without mirth. "At any rate Vero told me that I would have what she held when she died. But I received no word afterward, either from Mary or a lawyer, and then, reading that El Toro was rented to a stranger, I decided to go there myself to reclaim my own property."

"In what amounted to a disguise, Mrs. Adams?"

She said simply, "You could call it that, I suppose. Yes. You see I didn't want to be recognized by any former friends or neighbors, Inspector, for strictly personal reasons of my own. I can assure you they were not criminal reasons."

Then she turned to Hilliard. "You remember me, don't you, Henry?" she asked easily, her voice light. "I'm Alice."

Of the two she had by far the more aplomb. Hilliard had been standing motionless, staring at her bemused. He was completely off base, not even within reaching distance of the bag. As she spoke to him directly he came to with a start, passed a hand over his eyes, and blinked as though he were reorienting himself in a strange world. "Alice—of course . . . but—it's been a long time."

"Almost nineteen years."

"Yes."

A full stop there. Neither of them seemed to have

anything further to say to the other. Not, at least, McKee decided, while he was present. But he had accomplished his immediate purpose. Hilliard had been warned that his search of Veronica Dane's room at El Toro and his knocking out of Ward were on record. In view of that it wasn't likely that anything would happen to Ward now, in case the young fellow's memory should inconveniently return and he could recall his assailant. As for Mrs. Adams, she was going to be asked some embarrassing questions at the inquest in the morning. But she would smile and with her appearance and undoubted charm would probably get away with it. Had she come into the room on purpose after finding out he and Hilliard were in here? Perhaps to warn Hilliard, put a stop to any disclosures he might be going to make? It was impossible to say.

McKee left them together. He had other people to see, notably Jackson. He had had a word with a moody and disgruntled Steele when he reached the hotel and Steele had told him of Jackson's arrival. It would be interesting to see what the fat man would have to say for himself. McKee walked up the stairs and along a hall to the salesman's room. The murmur of voices came from behind the flimsy door. Two for the price of one? It could be no one else but Mrs. Fergusson.

When Jackson opened to his knock she wasn't visible. She had probably retreated into the next room through the connecting door or into the closet. It wasn't necessary to talk to her at the moment. If she couldn't hear, Jackson would give her a full report.

He received the Scotsman genially. "Ah, Inspector, thought I might see you . . . Take a chair. So you're stuck in this dump of a town like the rest of us. Oh well, I guess you gotta take the fat with the lean and it'll be over by tomorrow after this here inquest they're going to hold. Nuisance though, isn't it?"

His unabashed explanation of his departure from El

Toro in the small hours of the morning was that he couldn't sleep worrying about his ruined samples and how he was going to get more. Lying awake he had heard the wind change after a while and getting up and pulling on his clothes he had gone down to the front door for a look out. He was standing on the steps outside, trying to get a squint at the sky, when a boat had sailed practically up to his feet. It was a flat-bottomed rowboat. Without thinking he had jumped into it and with the one oar, the other one missing, he had poled his way to the road outside the gates and started walking in the direction of Albuquerque to see if he could get help. After a few miles an empty school bus had come along, and the driver had given him a lift down into the valley.

"And you went straight to the police?" McKee asked.

Jackson shook his head. He said it wasn't necessary. He was ravenous and he was in a beanery on the outskirts of the city when he saw first Mrs. Tafoya, and then that writer guy Steele, drive past the place hell bent for leather. They were both going lickety-split, so he knew everything was O.K. After his meal he had slept awhile in the joint with his head on the table until the waitress roused him. Then he had ambled here, to the only hotel in the town, to get a real good sleep in an honest to God bed.

McKee listened in silence to this rigmarole, most of it lies. Then he spoke.

"Would it interest you to know, Mr. Jackson, that Willie Stokes has been arrested and is in the hands of the state police?"

"*What . . .*" Jackson's mouth fell open. For a moment it reduced him to a pulp, a pale yellow quivering jelly. The room was far from hot but moisture beaded his forehead and jowls thickly. He wiped it off with a convulsive movement.

"My God, Willie stuck his neck out, did he, and the police grabbed him? . . . Is he in jail?"

McKee said yes, adding genially, "But I doubt he'll stay there very long. He's quite a lad. A man like that knows all the ropes and he'll be out on bail in practically no time at all."

Jackson tried to rally himself and started to bluster. What had he to do with Stokes? Nothing at all. He was an honest man and his slate was clean. Sure he was a friend of poor Etta, Willie's wife, he'd known her from a kid, and he had only been trying to help her. She was scared out of her wits of Willie, poor girl. That was the reason why she had come west to New Mexico as soon as she heard Willie was loose again. "She figured he wouldn't dare follow her out here as he was wanted in this state."

McKee contemplated the fat man thoughtfully. It wasn't his business to save either Jackson or Mrs. Fergusson's skin, but there had been enough bloodshed . . . Jackson's girth was still considerable but it had diminished slightly. He was no longer wearing the money belt. He had probably deposited the contents in a bank somewhere for the time being. The Scotsman said mildly, "Well, I thought I ought to warn you," and got out of his chair. "Stokes has already done some talking. He claims his wife, Mrs.—eh—Fergusson, appropriated his life's saving from a safe deposit box in New York without his authority or consent. I think that's what Stokes is after. If the stuff that was in the safe deposit box was handed over to him I doubt whether he'd make any further trouble."

McKee was at the door when the phone on a marble-topped table rang. It was the desk clerk. A Mr. Santander was in the lobby and would like a word with the Inspector as soon as was convenient.

"Inspector McKee?—Tony Santander." As the Scotsman came down the stairs Mr. Santander rose from his chair with a bow and shook hands ceremoniously after the manner of the Spanish. He was a small man with a magnificent brush of white hair, a dark skin, well-cut features and shrewd brown eyes. They assayed McKee appraisingly while he explained that when he called the state barracks, the man in charge there, Lieutenant Menendez, had suggested he talk to the Inspector at the Del Rio Grande where he was staying in order to be present at the inquest.

The two men moved to a couple of more distant chairs and sat down. Santander was deeply affected by Mary Dane's tragic death. He said, "I was always extremely fond of her. A dreadful thing. Terrible. That's why as soon as I heard I decided to go to the police." Sitting back and rolling a cigarette deftly he launched into his story.

At around eleven o'clock that morning he had had a long-distance call from a woman named Mrs. Ransom in Rosita, a small town some fifty miles away in the foothills of the Jemez Mountains.

"Ransom? Would that be young Ward's mother who worked for the Danes at El Toro years ago?" McKee asked.

Santander said he didn't know about Ward, but that Ward had been the name of Mrs. Ransom's first husband— and Mrs. Ransom had worked for the Danes for a considerable time when she was a girl.

Mrs. Ransom had been very much wrought up over the phone—and it wasn't because of Mary Dane's death, she didn't know about it until he told her. At any rate she wanted to see both the lawyer himself and Mrs. Adams immediately on an important matter.

"You know Mrs. Adams?"

Santander smiled. "Oh yes." He said he had known her since she was so high, and held a hand at knee-level palm down. She had been a very pretty child and she was now a handsome and charming woman with a lovely daughter of her own.

Mary and Veronica's niece lived in Santa Fe, but Santander had heard from the lieutenant at the barracks that she was coming to the Del Rio Grande to stay the night so as to be at the inquest to be held early the next morning. He had told Mrs. Ransom this over the phone and she said she would arrive on the bus that got in at five.

The lawyer looked at his watch. "I don't know what's keeping her. It's after half-past five now, and the bus station's just around the corner. But the bus may be late . . . I'd better go and call the station."

Santander got up. There was a phone booth near the foot of the stairs. He came back frowning. The Rosita bus had been on time. Mrs. Ransom must have missed it.

Mrs. Ransom hadn't missed the bus. The lawyer had hardly finished speaking when a woman screamed. It was a high scream of terror piercing in the shadowy quiet of the deserted lobby. The scream came from somewhere down the corridor to the right of the desk. Several public rooms opened off it, a library of sorts and the writing room. It was a maid, going into the writing room to empty the trash basket, who had given that shriek. What had forced it out of her was the body of a woman lying on the floor with blood all over her face.

The woman was Mrs. Ransom. There was no possible doubt about it. The lawyer, the Scotsman and the desk clerk were the first on the scene after the maid fled. Santander took a single glance at the figure on the carpet near one of the desks and nodded speechlessly.

"Dead?" he asked as McKee rose from his knees at the end of a brief examination.

"No perceptible pulse."

The clerk had hurried off and was already on the phone calling a Dr. Giles. The doctor was there within five minutes. Before he came the word had spread and the corridor outside was filled with people, crowding around the doorway and craning for a better view. Young Ward was among them. He must have heard something. McKee saw him forging a way through the huddle and into the room too late to stop him. He continued to advance until he caught sight of what lay on the floor. It jerked him to a halt.

"It's—yes, it's Mom," he cried in a loud voice, staring down and rubbing a hand aimlessly over his face. His mouth was working. He was dazed, incredulous.

Someone took hold of his arm. It was Hilliard. "Ward —come away. There's nothing you can do. The doctor will be here in a couple of minutes." He pushed Ward forcibly down the path that opened for them. When they were gone McKee closed the door firmly on a heterogeneous collection of staring faces.

Molly Ransom had been choked to death. Under the smeared blood her face was cyanotic, engorged. Santander was no longer gazing at her in horror. He was staring ahead of him at nothing, and he looked startled and thoughtful. He said after a moment and a deep sigh, "Who was that young fellow, Inspector?"

"Ward," McKee told him, "the boy I mentioned, Mrs. Ransom's son by her first marriage. Why do you ask?"

But the lawyer subtly retreated. "I just—wondered and I saw how affected he was. Must be a blow to him coming like this, poor fellow."

McKee was convinced that there was more to Santander's sudden sharp interest in Ward than that. Let it ride for the moment; he returned a frowning gaze to the woman at his feet. Something about the picture puzzled him, wasn't right. There was an incongruous note of some sort. Dr. Giles arrived then. Giles was also the coroner. He had oxygen with him, and various drugs. He gave Mrs. Ransom an injection, readjusted tubes and turned on the tank. They waited, silently watching.

McKee hadn't said so but he wasn't absolutely sure Mrs. Ransom was dead. He couldn't be. And she wasn't. She was almost gone but not quite. Another couple of minutes and it would have been too late. As it was, there was still a spark of life left. The killer had done his best. McKee reflected, thinking of the *reata* around Mary Dane's neck, that strangling was one of his favorite methods. In this case he hadn't succeeded completely.

It was going to be nip and tuck. While they waited the outcome of the injection and the oxygen Giles began asking questions. There was very little that was definite as far as the isolating of the perpetrator went, or could be at that point. Anyone in the hotel or anyone who had sighted Mrs. Ransom outside and followed her in could have done the job. On a pretext of some sort—"Just step in here for a moment"—the door closed, and then the attack. Hands around her throat, or she could have been strangled with the scarf she wore in disarray under the shabby black cloth coat.

Bending over to examine her throat more closely Giles gave a puzzled frown. "I can't understand the amount of blood . . . Some, yes, but not this much." McKee agreed promptly. That had given him pause, troubled him. Down on one knee again, Giles moved the head from side to side, raised it lightly, and gave an exclamation. "Something here."

He took a small forceps from his bag. The thing he drew out of Mrs. Ransom's throat was a heavy needle about four inches long. There was a bloodstained wisp of thread through an eye.

Santander looked sick, the doctor grim. McKee told them. The needle was the carpet needle Mrs. Fergusson had lost in the kitchen at El Toro up in the Sandias when her sewing basket had been upset, the needle that had vanished.

16

It was dark beyond the windows. The last stains of the March twilight were gone from the sky. McKee lay stretched out on a coverlet on a lumpy mattress in Steele's room on the second floor of the Hotel Del Rio Grande, his hands clasped behind his head, his eyes on a discolored patch of plaster on the ceiling. Steele stood at the basin, shaving.

More than two hours had passed since the finding of the carpet needle in Molly Ransom's throat and the Scotsman had done all that he could do about it himself afterwards. It depended now on what the local police found or didn't find in the various inquiries under way.

Dr. Giles, who as coroner would be conducting the inquest tomorrow, had been mystified by McKee's request for a snip of the bloodstained wool in the needle's eye, but he had complied after noting down the original length which was four inches. This scrap McKee had washed with loving care until the last trace of redness was gone from the beige which was its natural color. When Mrs. Fergusson had laid it down in the sewing basket in the hacienda there had been at least a good eighteen inches of it in the needle.

He had also pressed the Dane lawyer, Santander, hard. One of the details he had managed to get out of him with a considerable amount of effort was curious, and interesting. For nineteen years, ever since she left El Toro, Veronica Dane had been paying Mrs. Ransom a pension of a hundred dollars a month and in her will she had left her the sum of a thousand dollars outright. Mollie Ransom . . . M. for Molly, as in the note in Veronica's account book that said "the usual" was getting to be a drain and something would have to be done about it?

Mrs. Ransom had been twenty-five or twenty-six at the most when she left to marry her first husband Ward. True she had been with the Danes since she was a girl of sixteen, nevertheless you didn't usually pension a woman of that age off. McKee was something more than anxious to question her, but at the moment it was impossible. She was on the danger list and it was a tossup whether she'd live or die before she could speak and say what she had come down to the Del Rio Grande to say.

Other bits and pieces of information had come trickling in. After her stop at the house of the real Mrs. Tafoya in Albuquerque Mrs. Adams had returned home to Santa Fe. She had stayed there just long enough to put her daughter on a plane to New York to visit friends, to whom she herself had made a long-distance call as soon as she reached her house. After which Mrs. Adams had packed a bag, needless to say not the pasteboard affair she had carried as Mrs. Tafoya, and driven back here to the hotel in the Lincoln.

The Scotsman got off the bed and began to move around the room restlessly. It was almost eight o'clock. Twenty-four hours, neither more no less, was all they had until the next morning, at eight-thirty, in which to catch their fish. After the inquest all these people would be scattered and gone and the evidence of guilt, if there was any tangible evidence, would be destroyed or buried too deep to excavate. He said so. Running a comb through his wet hair in front of the spotted mirror, Steele grinned sourly at him.

"What do you care, Inspector? You stressed yourself up there at El Toro that once we were out of that god-forsaken mausoleum the whole thing would be off your neck and strictly the business of the New Mexico police."

McKee's smile was faintly sheepish. "I know, but I promised Lieutenant Menendez I'd do what I could as long as I was here. Besides, you hate to leave a case unresolved —and incidentally leave a murderer running around loose."

Steele shrugged. "Well, here's one baby won't be sorry to get out of New Mexico." He got into his coat and the two men left the bedroom. The corridor outside was broad, the strip of matting down the middle of it had replaced the carpeting of another era. Gloomy light came from what appeared to be ten-watt bulbs in sconces a considerable distance apart on the walls. The musty stillness was broken by Jill Sheppard's voice coming through a partially opened door a short distance away. "Yes, I did . . . No, I'm not going to marry Henry—I'm not going to marry anyone, ever." A stifled cry from Rita Mole. "Now Jill, you just can't—" She looked out, saw McKee and Steele, and the door closed with a bang.

McKee glanced at his companion. There was neither relief nor jubilation in him. He said acidly, "Miss Sheppard appears to have changed her mind again. It's evidently becoming a habit with her. I wonder who the next unlucky dog will be."

Ahead of them Ward was coming up the stairs, huddled down miserably in his shabby khaki windbreaker above dungarees tucked into his leather boots. His eyes were red-rimmed and his thin young face bore the marks of the terrific shock he had had that afternoon. He looked exhausted and forlorn. He had just been at the hospital to see his mother. But she was unconscious and they only let him see her for a moment.

He was about to pass on when Steele said, "What about a bite to eat, fellah?" And Ward said dully, looking down at mud-stained boots, "Thanks a lot, but I'm not hungry, Mr. Steele. Besides, in these clothes, in this kind of place . . ."

"All right, then we'll go somewhere else," Steele told him. "Come on, shake a leg. I want company anyhow and I'm starving. What about you, Inspector?"

McKee said he'd stay in the hotel, that messages would probably be coming through for him from New York, and they parted.

A faded, down-at-heel grandeur still persisted in the public rooms on the ground floor. They were large and spacious. The far end of the long dining room opening on a patio was brightly lighted and eight or nine tables there were set. Hilliard was alone at one of them sipping a cocktail. Two other places were laid; probably for the girl and Rita Mole. As he watched they joined him. If Miss Sheppard had meant what she had said to her sister upstairs and had already told Hilliard, there was no sign of it. They were all pleasant together.

There were no more than eight or nine other diners. Mrs. Fergusson, Mr. Jackson and Mrs. Adams were not among those present. McKee went into the little adjoining bar and had a couple of quick Scotches. Then he went back to the floor above. Mrs. Fergusson and Jackson weren't in their rooms. He reflected that the hotel dining room would be too public for them with Willie possibly out on bail and on the loose. Stepping out into the corridor from Jackson's room he stared. Mrs. Adams was proceeding away from him down the corridor. The room she had left was Henry Hilliard's.

As soon as she had disappeared around a corner he

went in—and found what he expected to find, a square envelope propped up on the ponderous bureau addressed to Hilliard. The envelope was sealed but the paste was still damp. He eased it up carefully, and read the enclosure fast. It was short and to the point. "I must see you tonight. It's imperative. I'll come to your room when the coast is clear."

So he had been right earlier. They had more to say to each other than they cared to say before witnesses or possible eavesdroppers. McKee put the note back and resealed the envelope quickly, running a balled fist over it, and went out. Downstairs in the dining room Mrs. Adams was seated at a small table against the wall with her back to the Hilliard party. McKee crossed the lobby to the phone booth and called the state barracks.

The check on all the people who had been incarcerated up at El Toro during the storm was still going on. There was nothing in yet. Then he called the hospital. No change. Mrs. Ransom was about the same except that her pulse was slightly lower. Her son was the only visitor she had had.

The Scotsman ate a sandwich and drank another Scotch in the bar and ordered coffee in the lobby from a morose waiter with an apparently permanent drop of moisture at the end of his nose, who appeared to have come with the foundations of the then fashionable spa. Presently Steele came in from the street and McKee waved to him. Steele was alone. Young Ward had gone back to the hospital. He sat down and told the ancient waiter to bring him a brandy. "This is a real whistle stop," he said. "I walked about a bit. I suppose the inquest's being held here because it's just over the line and in the same county as El Toro. Nothing new here I take it, from your expression."

McKee said no. The dining room was now empty of interest. Hilliard, the girl, Rita Mole and Mrs. Adams were gone and the room itself was now closed and darkened.

McKee's coffee was brought. He had finished it and was lighting a cigarette when he was called to the phone.

It was Lieutenant Menendez talking from the barracks. He had just had the word. The precautions the Scotsman had recommended had paid off. Five minutes earlier, shortly after she had been shifted to another room down the corridor, a succession of shots had been fired into the room from which Mrs. Ransom had been removed, by an assailant standing on a hillside less than twenty feet from the wide window and on a level with it. If she had been in the bed there she would almost certainly have been killed. The bullets had come from a Colt .38.

The only gun among the hacienda's late guests was Hilliard's in the glove compartment of his Rolls, parked in the lot across the street, and it was a Colt .38. Jackson had one but it was water-logged and useless. The gun was not in Hilliard's car. Someone had removed it. Nor was Hilliard in his room—which meant little or nothing, the others couldn't be located immediately either. And the hospital was less than five minutes' walk away.

Anyone could have taken the Colt from Hilliard's car, they all knew about it, just as anyone could have made a second and daring attempt to wipe out Mrs. Ransom a few minutes ago. The why was simple. To keep her from talking, the who remained very much up in the air.

The late occupants of El Toro were all back in the hotel within the next half-hour. None of them had been together. Mrs. Adams, Jill Sheppard and Hilliard had been walking about, each on his own. Rita Mole had been out strolling around the gardens. Jackson was also mobile at the time in question. He had sauntered back on foot from the Mexican joint where he had eaten; green chilis with scrambled eggs, and very good, too. Tasty. Mrs. Fergusson had eaten with him. She left the chili parlor a little earlier but he was in no hurry. The night was fine. Ward had been at the hospital and had come despondently back to the hotel. He hadn't been able to see his mother. The doctor was working with her. Willie Stokes remained among the absent.

It was almost half-past ten when bits of news began to come in from other lines out. Some of it was negative, some positive. The negative items were that the clothing Mrs. Adams had worn at the hacienda when she was there under the name of Tafoya showed no signs of rips that had been mended with the needle and woolen thread abstracted from Mrs. Fergusson's sewing basket. Neither did Miss Jill Sheppard's. That was as far as they had got with that angle.

Ward's story of his whereabouts in Albuquerque and his employment as a temporary in a lumber firm there before he started up into the Sandias on his trek south had been verified. Then came the positive statement.

Henry Hilliard had been at El Toro on the afternoon of the day Veronica Dane died. He had been seen and recognized riding in through the gates by a neighbor of the Danes driving past. He was on a big black horse and had apparently come over to the hacienda from his father's ranch six or seven miles to the east. McKee whistled softly. At the other end of the wire Lieutenant Menendez made no comment. The time was about 3:00 P.M. and Veronica Dane had died at the latest by four.

Menendez promised to phone whatever new came in as soon as it came in, no matter what the hour. In case the Inspector was busy elsewhere he was sending a trooper to the hotel to take messages and hand them over. It was ten minutes of eleven when McKee hung up. He remained as he was for the moment, his gaze absent on an Indian woman who had come into the lobby with a tray of silver trinkets and was being shooed off by the indignant clerk who was pointing at the clock over the desk. McKee left the booth. He had to hear and, if possible, see the interview between Hilliard and Mrs. Adams.

As things stood nothing conclusive or anywhere within shouting range of it had turned up. Meanwhile they were sitting on top of an active volcano, as witness those shots from the dark into the hospital room earlier that evening. Santander, the Dane lawyer, knew far more than he was admitting, but his professional lip was buttoned up and he wasn't going to talk—and they had to get light from somewhere.

The Scotsman had made some preparation; the rest would have to wait on opportunity and chance. The rooms in the old hotel were abnormally high-ceilinged and the tall doors had old-fashioned transoms over them. He had already found what he sought in a service closet in the corridor. It was a tall pole with a hook on the end of it for the opening and closing of transoms.

Using it he had opened the transom to Hilliard's room enough to hear through. The next thing, after Mrs. Adams' entrance, was a ladder. When Jones, the state trooper, appeared, McKee appealed to him and from somewhere or other Jones produced a stepladder, carried it up to the second floor by the service stairs, a narrow winding murderous trap, and placed it just around the corner from Hilliard's room. Other men were busy about a number of other things but after that as far as McKee was concerned there was nothing to do but wait.

17

By eleven-thirty the people under observation were all in their rooms and if not asleep at least most of their lights were out. It was devoutly to be hoped that they would stay put. It wasn't until almost ten minutes of one that Mrs. Adams finally materialized without noise in the dim corridor wearing a dark negligee. McKee watched her advance from the shelter of the broom closet. After a swift glance right and left she paused at Hilliard's door and tapped softly.

Hilliard was evidently waiting. The door opened at once and as soon as Mrs. Adams was through it, was then locked from the inside. Thirty seconds later the ladder was in place. McKee mounted the next to the top step. By moving the transom another cautious half-inch he could both see and hear what was going on in the room below him.

The curtains at the windows were tightly drawn and the only light came from a lamp on an elaborately carved marble-topped table in the middle of the floor with armchairs on either side of it. Mrs. Adams sat on the edge of one of them, hands clasped in front of her; Hilliard was in the other. They talked softly but their voices were perfectly audible at that distance and with no barrier intervening. Hilliard took out a case and offered her a cigarette. She waved it aside.

"No thanks, I want to get this over with . . . It's why I came back south again actually, to talk to you . . . I would have, even if the police hadn't found out who I was. But I don't think we ought to be any longer together than we have to." She paused for a moment and went on slowly.

"I won't go into what happened almost nineteen years ago, Henry. It's water over the dam . . . It was—pretty bad then. I thought at the time, there was nothing else for me to think, that you had deliberately abandoned me—I know better now, of course. Veronica intercepted our letters to each other and you never knew. You married someone else and after"—her voice took on a wry bitterness—"after I had the baby, I went away and tried to forget and finally did, and after another couple of years I married a good man. He's dead now. But I have a daughter, Eileen."

Hilliard nodded. He looked different. His gloss was gone. His face was almost haggard. He was strangely moved. "Yes, I know. Veronica told me when she summoned me to El Toro on the day on which she later died."

Mrs. Adams raised her eyes fully to his for the first time since she began to talk. Her faint smile was a mere shadow across her tenseness. She sat back in the chair. "Veronica wanted you to make an honest woman of me, didn't she, Henry?" He nodded and she went on, "A little late, wasn't she?—but she got very conscientious in her old age—or perhaps she still wanted to interfere . . . I don't know. She wrote asking me to go to El Toro on that day, too, but I had commitments and couldn't get away. She told me in her letter that—that our son would be there with his foster mother, Molly, the girl who used to work at El Toro. Molly had married and Veronica had persuaded her to adopt the boy as her son. But you know about that."

"Yes," Hilliard said, moistening his lips as though his mouth were dry. "I know. She told me when I went there that afternoon. She said she had our letters to each other, letters that she had intercepted, and the boy's birth certificate signed by the doctor who delivered him if I wanted proof, and that I could have them, on one condition."

"That you and I marry?"

"Yes. Veronica pointed out that my wife had died and your husband was dead and there was no longer any impediment between us. I needn't say I was astonished and —and overcome. It must have been hell for you at the time. Unspeakable hell. But—so many years had passed as you say—and I had just become engaged to Jill Sheppard . . . I told Veronica that what she proposed was impossible, out of the question, but I offered to do anything else she wanted for the boy, provide for him in any way she cared to name, if she'd give me those letters."

He paused and passed a hand briefly over his eyes. "Well, you know what she was like. She hated to be thwarted and she refused point-blank. She said I'd have my letters and the birth certificate when she died, and not until then. So"—he shrugged tiredly—"I left her. Then—and I didn't hear of it until much later—she did die that same afternoon. I waited. I thought the lawyer, Santander, would probably communicate with me after her death—but he didn't. I heard nothing whatever from anyone. So that last Wednesday when we found ourselves stranded near El Toro I decided to go there for the night and try and find the papers to which Veronica had alluded, our letters to each other and the birth certificate."

"And did you find them?"

"No."

"I thought not. I did the same thing you did myself. I searched, too. The only difference between us was that I went back to El Toro deliberately, as soon as I had heard through friends, who had gotten it from somewhere or other, that the ranch had been rented to a stranger and Mary had gone or was going away. You didn't recognize me as Mrs. Tafoya?"

Hilliard shook his head. "I was blind, I suppose. But I did recognize that young Ward was—our son, as soon as he spoke of his mother. Quite obviously he didn't know the truth and thought Molly actually was. I intend to provide for him. That goes without saying."

"I will help with that, Henry, I have plenty of money." When Hilliard started to object she put up a hand. "Since I—what shall I say?—grew up, I have bitterly regretted abandoning him, but I was very young at the time and very frightened and after his birth I was ill for a long while. Mary told me that the child was all right and in safe hands. It was enough for me . . . All I really wanted to do was to forget."

She sat up a little straighter. "When I left the hospital —instead of returning to El Toro I went to a friend of mine in New York—my father and mother were both dead. This friend had been an actress and ran a dramatic school. She and her husband thought I had talent. They got me spots and bit parts and I was on the stage for a year or so . . . No matter." She swept the past aside. "This is what I came to talk to you about. I think it would be much better if young Ward were never to know. It wouldn't do him any good and might only unsettle him. I'd rather he didn't know, ever. I have, as I told you, a daughter, an adolescent daughter, and the shock of—of finding this out about me—well, at her age I just don't want that to happen."

"I think I agree with you," Hilliard said slowly. "I can't see now that it would do young Ward much good to know the truth . . ."

"And no matter what happens, no matter what—you

won't say anything to anyone of what I've—what happened nineteen years ago?" Her voice was supplicating. In her eagerness she had risen to her feet, hands flat on the table leaning toward Hilliard.

The Scotsman stopped listening at the faintest of sounds off on the right. He turned his head. A trooper was advancing down the corridor in a hurry. McKee dropped to the floor. The trooper had news. He was talking quickly in a low voice when the door opened and Mrs. Adams came out.

She stopped dead at the sight of the two men. Finding them there was a frightful shock. Her glance touched the ladder, took in its significance. Nodding to the trooper who moved off at once, McKee said gravely, "I'd like to talk to both you and Mr. Hilliard, Mrs. Adams." Her breathing was rapid and she had gone very white but she made no demur, turning back into the room she had just left like a sleepwalker.

The Scotsman closed the door, and told them. What he had to say was rough. He said it fast in as few words as possible. Young Ward was their son—and Ward was a murderer. It was Ward who had killed both Gomez and Mary Dane. On that first night at the hacienda he was the one who had opened the cupboard in the dining room with the key he had taken from Mary's pocket and had removed the envelope addressed to the Dane lawyer—which was what Mary had returned to the hacienda to get.

Pain and heartbreak, they were both completely overcome, slain. Their son, born out of wedlock but nevertheless their son for all that, was a murderer. The blow was a crushing one. Frightful. And there were other things; there was no chance of escape for either of them, they couldn't get away, it would all have to come out into the open now . . .

McKee gave them time. Presently, after a long pause, Hilliard spoke. "How," he asked tonelessly in a dead voice, an elbow on the table, a hand shading his eyes, "how did he know—the truth, who he was? Not from Molly Ransom . . . ?"

"No," McKee said, "Mrs. Ransom kept the bargain she made with Veronica Dane to take the boy and rear him as her own. But he found out somehow, possibly by eavesdropping on his supposed mother and stepfather or perhaps listening to Mary Dane on one of Miss Dane's infrequent visits to Mrs. Ransom. At any rate he was at El Toro on the day you went there to see Veronica in reply to her summons."

McKee felt for a cigarette and dropped the pack back untouched. He said, "Requestioned a couple of hours ago, the neighbor driving past who saw you at the Dane ranch that day also saw a young man answering Ward's description making for the Dane gates and turning through them on foot practically on your heels. There's not much doubt that hidden somewhere he listened to you and Veronica talk. Then he was sure. After he finally got the documents the other night he sewed them into the sheepskin lining of his coat with the darning needle he stole from Mrs. Fergusson's sewing basket at the hacienda, the needle that he thrust deep into Mrs. Ransom's throat to try and make sure of her death."

A deep shudder went through Mrs. Adams, otherwise motionless in her chair. But she didn't speak, nor did Hilliard. McKee went on. "In all probability, after you left the hacienda that afternoon he came out of hiding, confronted Veronica Dane threateningly, and demanded the documents. Whether she died of shock and fear or whether he attacked her is a moot point. In any event, she did die, and at the arrival of Mary Dane—according to the evidence she got back to El Toro within minutes of her sister's death—Ward fled after shooting the Dalmatian who must have followed him barking. Ward didn't go far. He remained within reaching distance, he got a job in Albuquerque and waited for a chance to make a further search for the documents he wanted—and then he read of the renting of El Toro."

Lieutenant Menendez was questioning Ward in a room down the corridor. There were a number of details the Scotsman was curious about, first and foremost among them the question of why Ward had tried to kill his foster mother. He said, "I'll be back later." He might as well have been talking to the empty air. Neither Hilliard nor Mrs. Adams answered. They scarcely seemed to hear him. He left the room quietly and went along the hall and around the corner.

Ward was there, in a chair against the wall. He was white under the freckles but it was surprising to see how boyish and almost shy he looked. Engaging. Nature had given him an almost perfect mask. Even now it was difficult to believe that behind that appealing front he was a ruthless killer. But under Menendez's probing he was cold, unflurried and calculating. His reiterated denial to the lieutenant, a blanket denial, was a neat display of injured innocence.

The gist of it was, "So you police entered my room with a passkey while I was asleep here tonight and took my coat and found papers sewed in the lining with a certain kind of thread. I don't know anything about that. I didn't put any papers there." He hadn't killed Mary, he hadn't killed Gomez. He hadn't tried to kill his mother, whom he loved. "Why should I?"

Watching him McKee thought musingly of Molly Ransom's trip down here to see the lawyer and Alice Adams, nee Dane—of Ward's attack on her as soon as she arrived at the hotel . . . The glimmering of an idea began to dawn at the back of his mind. It could be . . . It was at least possible . . .

Menendez continued to probe at Ward relentlessly. The Scotsman went downstairs and called the hospital.

Mrs. Ransom's condition was slightly improved. Pulse and respiration were steadier. She had opened her eyes for a moment and muttered a few words. Her chances of recovery were a little better.

McKee hung up. There were half a dozen things to be done at once. He left the hotel. It was then after 1:00 P.M. He called the barracks again. Hilliard's room was dark. So was Mrs. Adams'. He felt sorry for them both—a youthful error, nineteen or twenty years old, had brought utter tragedy down on their heads when they had put it safely behind them and it was probably only a dim memory. The real culprit was Veronica Dane playing the almighty with the lives of the people about her.

It was just five-thirty when he reëntered the sprawling structure and went upstairs to Steele's room. The light was gray; the sun wouldn't appear behind the Sandias for another hour. Steele wasn't asleep. He was up and dressed and slinging shirts and his shaving kit into his bag.

Late the night before his car had been righted and brought to the hotel parking lot by men from the sheriff's office. As soon as the inquest was over he meant to head east.

"Those damn birds," he said. "What a racket. The first one, the guy that woke the bugler up began at twenty after four."

McKee didn't believe it was the birds that had cut Steele's sleep short. Dousing his head in a basin of cold water and toweling it vigorously, he said he, too, was leaving by plane in an hour or so because there would be no inquest. He told the younger man, briefly, about Ward. There was no time for more. He had to see Hilliard and Mrs. Adams for a final word.

Shoveling into his jacket and then into his topcoat he said, "Tell you all about it in New York," and made for the door. On the threshold he added offhandedly, "Oh, by the way, I shoved that letter to you from Miss Sheppard's brother-in-law under her door last night. If you want it back you can get it from her," and closed the door behind him.

He went to Hilliard's room first. Opening to his tap Hilliard put a finger to his lips. To McKee's surprise Mrs. Adams was still there, in the chair in front of the table, her head on the crook of an arm. She had evidently been there all night. She was deeply asleep.

Hilliard said softly, "We talked until very late and she's dead tired." His face was gray, hopeless. At the sound of voices Mrs. Adams woke with a start and sat up. She stared from one man to the other as though expecting another blow.

"What is it?" she said faintly. Then as she saw something new in the Scotsman's face, her own lit up. "You found out that—that young man (it was the nearest she could get to Ward) *isn't* guilty . . ."

McKee shook his head. "The man calling himself Ward is guilty all right, Mrs. Adams, only—he is not your son."

A stunned pause. They both stared at him uncomprehendingly. He went on talking. He said that the young man who had called himself Ward was George Ransom, Mrs. Ransom's stepson, her second husband's son by a previous marriage. Their own son was dead. He had died in an accident when he was fifteen years old. Molly Ransom and her husband had continued to collect the hundred a month from Veronica Dane for some four years. For all his engaging manners George Ransom, to give him his proper name, was never much good. In fact he was a thoroughly bad egg. He had been arrested on suspicion of a car theft at the age of seventeen and his fingerprints had been taken. That was how the police had finally, at three o'clock that morning, unearthed his real identity.

Slow tears were rolling down Mrs. Adams' face. Hilliard said, "Good God," on a spent breath.

Easy enough, knowing the facts, the Scotsman said, to

see how the boy had found out the truth. Listening to his father and his stepmother, examining mail, etcetera. And then he had probably read the letter from Veronica Dane ordering his mother to bring her foster son to the hacienda on the day she herself died. Veronica's intention had evidently been to confront both her niece and Hilliard with their son.

But her own plans had gone awry. Mrs. Ransom was afraid to go to El Toro. She couldn't take her stepson there and produce him as a stand-in for the dead boy because Mary Dane, who had paid her several visits over the years, would have recognized the deception at once. So Mrs. Ransom's husband had written Veronica Dane a note saying that his wife was in Arizona visiting a sick friend. In the hospital, semiconscious for a second or so at around 2:00 A.M., Molly Ransom had uttered a few incoherent words. McKee quoted them verbatim.

"Not Peter. Not Peter . . . I—"

He explained. It was the selfsame sentence, or part of it, that Gomez had managed to get out when he was dying. What Gomez had undoubtedly been doing was quoting Mary. He had seen the confrontation between young Ransom and Mary in the stable through the broken window at the back. What had happened was that Mary had said, "You're not Peter," when Ransom tried to bluff her—and so had died. By the time Gomez got around to the stables it was too late. Mary's body was being covered with straw. Gomez had started for the hacienda at top speed to get help there. And Ransom had caught up with him in the courtyard and had struck that lethal blow, probably with a billet of wood. The rest of what had happened at El Toro they knew.

"I don't see," Hilliard said slowly after McKee finished, "what his final objective was."

"That's simple enough," McKee told him. "He's a shrewd lad. You were about to remarry and he knew that in any case you wouldn't want the truth to come out, so what he intended to do at his leisure was either to blackmail you with your letters and the birth certificate or present himself to you as your son—whichever seemed the more advantageous."

Some of the despair had returned to Mrs. Adams' exhausted face. Her main concern was still her daughter. "I suppose the whole truth will have to come out at the trial?"

The Scotsman shook his head. "There won't be any trial," he said. "As young Ransom was being put into a cell, tricky to the last, he managed to snatch the trooper's gun. In the struggle for it he was fatally shot."

She gave a low cry of unutterable relief but there was pain in it, too. McKee said, "No, Mrs. Adams, I think you'll find Lieutenant Menendez coöperative." As he spoke he looked through the window beyond her, the room faced the street.

Steele was out there at the wheel of his car. And someone was flying down the path toward him. It was Jill Sheppard and she was carrying a bag. From far away a thin voice cried, "Jill." It was Rita Mole. It didn't stop the girl. She had the car door open and was inside of it. The next moment it shot forward out of sight.

The two people inside the room were oblivious. They would carry scars for the rest of their lives. But the worst was over for them. Mrs. Adams' eyes were full of tears. She buried her face in her folded arms. "It was all my fault— three deaths . . . I shouldn't have abandoned the child— my fault, my fault."

Hilliard had recovered some of his former vigor. "No, Alice," he said vehemently, "no, Alice, no. That's not so. It was Veronica's fault, from the beginning, and hers alone," and laid a hand gently on Alice Adams' hair.

His work there was finished; without another word McKee left the room and the hotel. Thirty-five minutes later he was airborne with the nose of the great plane pointed east.

ABOUT THE AUTHOR

HELEN REILLY, whose death occurred shortly after completion of this, her thirty-fourth novel, was a noted practitioner of the suspense genre. The lasting popularity of her work owes much to her ingenious plotting, her clever use of police techniques, and, far from least, her creation of that astute Scotsman, Inspector McKee. Though in command of Manhattan Homicide, McKee's nimble detection has often snared elusive killers in remote places.

Mrs. Reilly grew up in New York City, where her father, Dr. James Michael Kieran, was president of Hunter College. She herself received her education there until she married the late Paul Reilly, artist-cartoonist. Her brother, John Kieran, is the distinguished sports writer and naturalist. Ursula Curtiss, the well-known mystery writer, is her daughter. Mrs. Reilly was an active member, and past president, of the Mystery Writers of America. In recent years she made her home in New Mexico.